Gilbert Parker

The Translation of a Savage

Gilbert Parker

**The Translation of a Savage**

ISBN/EAN: 9783337312923

Printed in Europe, USA, Canada, Australia, Japan

Cover: Foto ©Andreas Hilbeck / pixelio.de

More available books at **www.hansebooks.com**

BY

# GILBERT PARKER

AUTHOR OF

"PIERRE AND HIS PEOPLE," "THE CHIEF FACTOR.
"MRS. FALCHION," ETC.

TORONTO:

THE COPP, CLARK COMPANY, LIMITED

# CONTENTS

# TRANSLATION OF A SAVAGE

## CHAPTER I

### HIS GREAT MISTAKE

IT appeared that Armour had made the great
mistake of his life. When people came to know,
they said that to have done it when sober had
shown him possessed of a kind of maliciousness
and cynicism almost pardonable, but to do it
when tipsy proved him merely weak and foolish.
But the fact is, he was less tipsy at the time than
was imagined ; and he could have answered to
more malice and cynicism than was credited to
him. To those who know the world it is not
singular that, of the two, Armour was thought
to have made the mistake and had the misfortune, or that people wasted their pity and
their scorn upon him alone. Apparently they

7

did not see that the woman was to be pitied. He had married her ; and she was only an Indian girl from Fort Charles of the Hudson's Bay Company, with a little honest white blood in her veins. Nobody, not even her own people, felt that she had anything at stake, or was in danger of unhappiness, or was other than a person who had ludicrously come to bear the name of Mrs. Francis Armour. If any one had said in justification that she loved the man, the answer would have been that plenty of Indian women had loved white men, but had not married them, and yet the population oi half-breeds went on increasing.

Frank Armour had been a popular man in London. His club might be found in the vicinity of Pall Mall, his father's name was high and honoured in the Army List, one of his brothers had served with Wolseley 'n Africa, and Frank himself, having no profession, but with a taste for business and investment, had gone to Canada with some such intention as Lord Selkirk's in the early part of the century. He owned large shares in the Hudson's Bay Company, and when he travelled through the North-West country, prospecting, he was received most hospitably. Of an inquiring and gregarious nature he went as much among the half-breeds—or métis, as they are called—and

Indians as among the officers of the Hudson's
Bay Company and the white settlers. He had
ever been credited with having a philosophical
turn of mind; and this was accompanied by a
certain strain of impulsiveness or daring. He
had been accustomed all his life to make up his
mind quickly, and, because he was well enough
off to bear the consequences of momentary
rashness in commercial investments, he was
not counted among the transgressors. He had
his own fortune; he was not drawing upon a
common purse. It was a different matter when
he trafficked rashly in the family name so far
as to marry the daughter of Eye-of-the-Moon,
the Indian chief.

He was tolerably happy when he went to the
Hudson's Bay country; for Miss Julia Sherwood
was his promised wife, and she, if poor, was
notably beautiful and of good family. His
people had not looked quite kindly on this
engagement; they had, indeed, tried in many
ways to prevent it; partly because of Miss
Sherwood's poverty, and also because they
knew that Lady Agnes Martling had long cared
for him, and was most happily endowed with
wealth and good looks also. When he left for
Canada they were inwardly glad (they imagined
that something might occur to end the engagement)—all except Richard, the wiseacre of the

9

family, the book-man, the drone, who preferred living at Greyhope, their Hertfordshire home, the year through, to spending half the time in Cavendish Square. Richard was very fond of Frank, admiring him immensely for his buxom strength and cleverness, and not a little, too, for that very rashness which had brought him such havoc at last.

Richard was not, as Frank used to say, "perfectly sound on his pins,"—that is, he was slightly lame,—but he was right at heart. He was an immense reader, but made little use of what he read. He had an abundant humour, and remembered every anecdote he ever heard. He was kind to the poor, walked much, talked to himself as he walked, and was known by the humble sort as "a 'centric." But he had a wise head, and he foresaw danger to Frank's happiness when he went away. While others had gossiped and manœuvred and were busily idle, he had watched things. He saw that Frank was dear to Julia in proportion to the distance between her and young Lord Haldwell, whose father had done something remarkable in guns or torpedoes and was rewarded with a lordship and an uncommonly large fortune. He also saw that, after Frank left, the distance between Lord Haldwell and Julia became distinctly less —they were both staying at Greyhope. Julia

Sherwood was a remarkably clever girl. Though he felt it his duty to speak to her for his brother, —a difficult and delicate matter,—he thought it would come better from his mother.

But when he took action it was too late. Miss Sherwood naïvely declared that she had not known her own heart, and that she did not care for Frank any more. She wept a little, and was soothed by motherly Mrs. Armour, who was inwardly glad, though she knew the matter would cause Frank pain; and even General Armour could not help showing slight satisfaction, though he was innocent of any deliberate action to separate the two. Straightway Miss Sherwood despatched a letter to the wilds of Canada, and for a week was an unengaged young person. But she was no doubt consoled by the fact that for some time past she had had complete control of Lord Haldwell's emotions. At the end of the week her perceptions were justified by Lord Haldwell's proposal, which, with admirable tact and obvious demureness, was accepted.

Now, Frank Armour was wandering much in the wilds, so that his letters and papers went careering about after him, and some that came first were last to reach him. That was how he received a newspaper announcing the marriage of Lord Haldwell and Julia Sherwood at the same time that her letter, written in estimable English and with admirable feeling, came, begging for a release from their engagement, and, towards its close, assuming, with a charming regret, that all was over, and that the last word had been said between them.

Armour was sitting in the trader's room at Fort Charles when the carrier came with the mails. He had had some successful days hunting buffalo with Eye-of-the-Moon and a little band of métis, had had a long *pow-wow* in Eye-of-the-Moon's lodge, had chatted gaily with Lali the daughter, and was now prepared to enjoy heartily the arrears of correspondence and news before him. He ran his hand through the letters and papers, intending to classify them immediately, according to such handwriting as he recognised and the dates on the envelopes. But, as he did so, he saw a newspaper from which the wrapper was partly torn. He also saw a note in the margin directing him to a certain page. The note was in Richard's handwriting. He opened the paper at the page indicated and saw the account of the marriage! His teeth clinched on his cigar, his face turned white, the paper fell from his fingers. He gasped, his hands spread out nervously, then caught the table and held it as though to steady himself.

The trader rose. "You are ill," he said,

"Have you bad news?" He glanced towards the paper.

Slowly Armour folded the paper up, and then rose unsteadily. "Gordon," he said, "give me a glass of brandy."

He turned towards the cupboard in the room. The trader opened it, took out a bottle, and put it on the table beside Armour, together with a glass and some water. Armour poured out a stiff draught, added a very little water, and drank it. He drew a great sigh, and stood looking at the paper.

"Is there anything I can do for you, Mr. Armour?" urged the trader.

"Nothing, thank you, nothing at all. Just leave the brandy here, will you? I feel knocked about, and I have to go through the rest of these letters."

He ran his fingers through the pile, turning it over hastily, as if searching for something. The trader understood. He was a cool-headed Scotsman ; he knew that there were some things best not inquired into, and that men must have their bad hours alone. He glanced at the brandy debatingly, but presently turned and left the room in silence. In his own mind, however, he wished he might have taken the brandy without being discourteous. Armour had discovered Miss Sherwood's letter. Before he

13

opened it he took a little more brandy. Then
he sat down and read it deliberately. The
liquor had steadied him. The fingers of one
hand even drummed on the table. But the face
was drawn, the eyes were hard, and the look of
him was altogether pinched. After he had
finished this, he looked for others from the same
hand. He found none. Then he picked out
those from his mother and father. He read
them grimly. Once he paused as he read his
mother's letter, and took a gulp of plain brandy.
There was something very like a sneer on his
face when he finished reading. He read the
hollowness of the sympathy extended to him ;
he understood the far from adroit references to
Lady Agnes Martling. He was very bitter.
He opened no more letters, but took up the
*Morning Post* again, and read it slowly through.
The look of his face was not pleasant. There
was a small looking-glass opposite him. He
caught sight of himself in it. He drew his hand
across his eyes and forehead, as though he was
in a miserable dream. He looked again ; he
could not recognise himself.

He then bundled the letters and papers into
his despatch-box. His attention was drawn to
one letter. He picked it up. It was from
Richard. He started to break the seal, but
paused. The strain of the event was too much ;

he winced. He determined not to read it then, to wait until he had recovered himself. He laughed now painfully. It had been better for him—it had, maybe, averted what people were used to term his tragedy — had he read his brother's letter at that moment. For Richard Armour was a sensible man, notwithstanding his peculiarities; and perhaps the most sensible words he ever wrote were in that letter thrust unceremoniously into Frank Armour's pocket.

Armour had received a terrible blow. He read his life backwards. He had no future. The liquor he had drunk had not fevered him, it had not wildly excited him ; it merely drew him up to a point where he could put a sudden impulse into practice without flinching. He was bitter against his people ; he credited them with more interference than was actual. He felt that happiness had gone out of his life and left him hopeless. As we said, he was a man of quick decisions. He would have made a dashing but reckless soldier ; he was not without the elements of the gamester. It is possible that there was in him also a strain of cruelty, undeveloped but radical. Life so far had evolved the best in him ; he had been cheery and candid. Now he travelled back into new avenues of his mind and found strange, aboriginal passions, fully adapted to the present

15

situation. Vulgar anger and reproaches were not after his nature. He suddenly found sources of refined but desperate retaliation. He drew upon them. He would do something to humiliate his people and the girl who had spoiled his life. Some one thing! It should be absolute and lasting, it should show how low had fallen his opinion of women, of whom Julia Sherwood had once been chiefest to him. In that he would show his scorn of her. He would bring down the pride of his family, who, he believed, had helped, out of mere selfishness, to tumble his happiness into the shambles.

He was older by years than an hour ago. But he was not without the faculty of humour, that was why he did not become very excited ; it was also why he determined upon a comedy which should have all the elements of tragedy. Perhaps, however, he would have hesitated to carry his purposes to immediate conclusions, were it not that the very gods seemed to play his game with him. For, while he stood there, looking out into the yard of the fort, a Protestant missionary passed the window. The Protestant missionary, as he is found at such places as Fort Charles, is not a strictly superior person. A Jesuit might have been of advantage to Frank Armour at that moment. The Protestant missionary is not above comfortable assurances

of gold. So that when Armour summoned this
one in, and told him what was required of him,
and slipped a generous gift of the Queen's coin
into his hand, he smiled vaguely and was
willing to do what he was bidden. Had he
been a Jesuit, who is sworn to poverty, and more
often than not a man of birth and education, he
might have influenced Frank Armour and prevented the notable mishap and scandal. As it
was, Armour took more brandy.

Then he went down to Eye-of-the-Moon's
lodge. A few hours afterwards the missionary
met him there. The next morning Lali, the
daughter of Eye-of-the-Moon, and the chieftainess of a portion of her father's tribe, whose
grandfather had been a white man, was introduced to the Hudson's Bay country as Mrs.
Frank Armour. But that was not all. Indeed,
as it stood, it was very little. He had only
made his comedy possible as yet; now the
play itself was to come. He had carried his
scheme through boldly so far. He would not
flinch in carrying it out to the last letter. He
brought his wife down to the Great Lakes
immediately, scarcely resting night or day.
There he engaged an ordinary but reliable
woman, to whom he gave instructions, and
sent the pair to the coast. He instructed his
solicitor at Montreal to procure passages for

B                            17

Mrs. Francis Armour and maid for Liverpool. Then, by letters, he instructed his solicitor in London to meet Mrs. Francis Armour and maid at Liverpool and take them to Greyhope in Hertfordshire—that is, if General Armour and Mrs. Armour, or some representative of the family, did not meet them when they landed from the steamship. .

Presently he sat down and wrote to his father and mother, and asked them to meet his wife and her maid when they arrived by the steamer *Aphrodite.* He did not explain to them in precise detail his feelings on Miss Julia Sherwood's marriage, nor did he go into full particulars as to the personality of Mrs. Frank Armour; but he did say that, because he knew they were anxious that he should marry "acceptably," he had married into the aristocracy, the oldest aristocracy, of America; and because he also knew they wished him to marry wealth, he sent them a wife rich in virtues—native, unspoiled virtues. He hoped that they would take her to their hearts and cherish her. He knew their firm principles of honour, and that he could trust them to be kind to his wife until he returned to share the affection which he was sure would be given to her. It was not his intention to return to England for some time yet. He had work to do in connection with his proposed colony ; and a wife—even a native wife—could not well be a companion in the circumstances. Besides, Lali—his wife's name was Lali!—would be better occupied in learning the peculiarities of the life in which her future would be cast. It was possible they would find her an apt pupil. Of this they could not complain, that she was untravelled ; for she had ridden a horse, bareback, half across the continent. They could not cavil at her education, for she knew several languages—aboriginal languages—of the North. She had merely to learn the dialect of English society, and how to carry with acceptable form the costumes of the race to which she was going. Her own costume was picturesque, but it might appear unusual in London society. Still, they could use their own judgment about that.

Then, when she was gone beyond recall, he chanced one day to put on the coat he wore when the letters and paper declaring his misfortune came to him. He found his brother's letter; he opened it and read it. It was the letter of a man who knew how to appreciate at their proper value the misfortunes, as the fortunes, of life. While Frank Armour read he came to feel for the first time that his brother Richard had suffered, maybe, from some such misery as had come to him through

19

Julia Sherwood. It was a dispassionate, manly letter, relieved by a gentle wit, and hinting with careful kindness that a sudden blow was better for a man than a lifelong thorn in his side. Of Julia Sherwood he had nothing particularly bitter to say. He delicately suggested that she had acted according to her nature, and that in the seesaw of life Frank had had a sore blow; but this was to be borne. The letter did not say too much; it did not magnify the difficulty, it did not depreciate it. It did not even directly counsel; it was wholesomely, tenderly judicial. Indirectly it dwelt upon the steadiness and manliness of Frank's character; directly, lightly, and without rhetoric, it enlarged upon their own comradeship. It ran over pleasantly the days of their boyhood, when they were hardly ever separated. It made distinct, yet with no obvious purpose, how good were friendship and confidence— which might be the most unselfish thing in the world—between two men. With the letter before him Frank Armour saw his act in a new light.

As we said, it is possible if he had read it on the day when his trouble came to him, he had not married Lali, or sent her to England on this—to her—involuntary mission of revenge. It is possible, also, that there came to him the first vague conception of the wrong he had done this Indian girl, who undoubtedly married him because she cared for him after her heathen fashion, while he had married her for nothing that was commendable ; not even for passion, which may be pardoned, nor for vanity, which has its virtues. He had had his hour with circumstance; circumstance would have its hour with him in due course. Yet there was no extraordinary revulsion. He was still angry, cynical, and very sore. He would see the play out with a consistent firmness. He almost managed a smile when a letter was handed to him some weeks later, bearing his solicitor's assurance that Mrs. Frank Armour and her maid had been safely bestowed on the *Aphrodite* for England. This was the first act in his tragic comedy.

# CHAPTER II

## A DIFFICULT SITUATION

WHEN Mrs. Frank Armour arrived at Montreal she still wore her Indian costume of clean, well-broidered buckskin, moccasins, and leggings, all surmounted by a blanket. It was not a distinguished costume, but it seemed suitable to its wearer. Mr. Armour's agent was in a quandary. He had received no instructions regarding her dress. He felt, of course, that, as Mrs. Frank Armour, she should put off these garments, and dress, so far as was possible, in accordance with her new position. But when he spoke about it to Mackenzie, the elderly maid and companion, he found that Mr. Armour had said that his wife was to arrive in England dressed as she was. He saw something ulterior in the matter, but it was not his province to interfere. And so Mrs. Frank Armour was a passenger by the *Aphrodite* in her buckskin garments.

What she thought of it all is not quite easy

to say. It is possible that at first she only considered that she was the wife of a white man,—
a thing to be desired,—and that the man she
loved was hers for ever—a matter of indefinable
joy to her. That he was sending her to England
did not fret her, because it was his will, and he
knew what was best. Busy with her contented
and yet somewhat dazed thoughts of him,—she
was too happy to be very active mentally, even
if it had been the characteristic of her race,—she
was not at first aware how much notice she
excited, and how strange a figure she was in
this staring city. When it did dawn upon her
she shrank a little, but still was placid, preferring
to sit with her hands folded in her lap, idly
watching things. She appeared oblivious that
she was the wife of a man of family and rank ;
she was only thinking that the man was hers—
all hers. He had treated her kindly enough in
the days they were together, but she had not
been a great deal with him, because they
travelled fast, and his duties were many, or he
made them so—but the latter possibility did
not occur to her.

When he had hastily bidden her farewell at
Port Arthur he had kissed her and said, " Good-
bye, my wife." She was not yet acute enough
in the inflections of Saxon speech to catch the
satire — almost involuntary — in the last two

words. She remembered the words, however, and the kiss, and she was quite satisfied. To what she was going she did not speculate. He was sending her: that was enough.

The woman given to her as maid had been well chosen. Armour had done this carefully. She was Scotch, was reserved, had a certain amount of shrewdness, would obey instructions, and do her duty carefully. What she thought about the whole matter she kept to herself; even the solicitor at Montreal could not find out. She had her instructions clear in her mind; she was determined to carry them out to the letter,—for which she was already well paid, and was like to be better paid; because Armour had arranged that she should continue to be with his wife after they got to England. She understood well the language of Lali's tribe, and because Lali's English was limited she would be indispensable in England.

Mackenzie, therefore, had responsibility, and if she was not elated over it, she still knew the importance of her position, and had enough practical vanity to make her an efficient servant and companion. She already felt that she had got her position in life, from which she was to go out no more for ever. She had been brought up in the shadow of Alnwick Castle, and she knew what was due to her charge—by other people ; herself only should have liberty with her. She was taking Lali to the home of General Armour, and that must be kept constantly before her mind. Therefore, from the day they set foot on the *Aphrodite*, she kept her place beside Mrs. Armour, sitting with her, —they walked very little,—and scarcely ever speaking, either to her or to the curious passengers. Presently the passengers became more inquisitive, and made many attempts at being friendly ; but these received little encouragement. It had become known who the Indian girl was, and many wild tales went about as to her marriage with Francis Armour. Now it was maintained she had saved his life at an outbreak of her tribe ; again, that she had found him dying in the woods and had nursed him back to life and health ; yet again, that she was a chieftainess, a successful claimant against the Hudson's Bay Company—and so on.

There were several on board who knew the Armours well by name, and two who knew them personally. One was Mr. Edward Lambert, a barrister of the Middle Temple, and the other was Mrs. Townley, a widow, a member of a well-known Hertfordshire family, who, on a pleasant journey in Scotland, had met, conquered, and married a wealthy young American, and had been left alone in the world, by no means portionless, eighteen months before. Lambert knew Richard Armour well, and when, from Francis Armour's solicitor, with whom he was acquainted, he heard, just before they started, who the Indian girl was, he was greatly shocked and sorry. He guessed at once the motive, the madness, of this marriage. But he kept his information and his opinions mostly to himself, except in so far as it seemed only due to friendship to contradict the numberless idle stories going about. After the first day at sea he came to know Mrs. Townley, and when he discovered that they had many common friends and that she knew the Armours, he spoke a little more freely to her regarding the Indian wife, and told her what he believed was the cause of the marriage.

Mrs. Townley was a woman—a girl—of uncommon gentleness of disposition, and, in spite of her troubles, inclined to view life with a sunny eye. She had known of Frank Armour's engagement with Miss Julia Sherwood, but she had never heard the sequel. If this was the sequel—well, it had to be faced. But she was almost tremulous with sympathy when she remembered Mrs. Armour, and Frank's gay, fashionable sister, Marion, and contemplated the arrival of this Indian girl at Greyhope. She had always liked Frank Armour, but this made her angry with him ; for, on second thoughts, she was not more sorry for him and for his people than for Lali, the wife. She had the true instinct of womanhood, and she supposed that a heathen like this could have feelings to be hurt and a life to be wounded as herself or another. At least she saw what was possible in the future when this Indian girl came to understand her position—only to be accomplished by contact with the new life, so different from her past. Both she and Lambert decided that she was very fine-looking, notwithstanding her costume. She was slim and well built, with modest bust and shapely feet and ankles. Her eyes were large, meditative, and intelligent, her features distinguished. She was a goodly product of her race, being descended from a line of chiefs and chieftainesses—broken only in the case of her grandfather, as has been mentioned. Her hands (the two kindly inquisitors decided) were almost her best point. They were perfectly made, slim yet plump, the fingers tapering, the wrist supple. Mrs. Townley then and there decided that the girl had possibilities. But here she was, an Indian, with few signs of civilisation or of that breeding which seems to white people the only breeding fit for earth or heaven.

Mrs. Townley did not need Lambert's suggestion that she should try to approach the girl,

27

make friends with her, and prepare her in some
slight degree for the strange career before her.

Mrs. Townley had an infinite amount of tact.
She knew it was best to approach the attendant first. This she did, and, to the surprise of
other lady-passengers, received no rebuff. Her
advance was not, however, rapid. Mackenzie
had had her instructions. When, she found that
Mrs. Townley knew Francis Armour and his
people, she thawed a little more, and then, very
hesitatingly, she introduced her to the Indian
wife. Mrs. Townley smiled her best—and there
were many who knew how attractive she could
be at such a moment. There was a slight
pause, in which Lali looked at her meditatively,
earnestly, and then those beautiful wild fingers
glided out, and caught her hand, and held it;
but she spoke no word. She only looked inquir-
ingly, seriously, at her new-found friend, and
presently dropped the blanket away from her,
and sat up firmly, as though she felt she was
not altogether an alien now, and had a right to
hold herself proudly among white people, as she
did in her own country and with her own tribe,
who had greatly admired her. Certainly Mrs.
Townley could find no fault with the woman
as an Indian. She had taste, carried her clothes
well, and was superbly fresh in appearance
though her hair still bore very slight traces of

the grease which even the most aristocratic Indians use.

But Lali would not talk. Mrs. Townley was anxious that the girl should be dressed in European costume, and offered to lend and rearrange dresses of her own, but she came in collision with Mr. Armour's instructions. So she had to assume a merely kind and comforting attitude. The wife had not the slightest idea where she was going, and even when Mackenzie, at Mrs. Townley's oft-repeated request, explained very briefly and unpicturesquely, she only looked incredulous or unconcerned. Yet the ship, its curious passengers, the dining-saloon, the music, the sea, and all, had given her suggestions of what was to come. They had expected that at table she would be awkward and ignorant to a degree. But she had at times eaten at the trader's table at Fort Charles, and had learned how to use a knife and fork. She had also been a favourite with the trader's wife, who had taught her very many civilised things. Her English, though far from abundant, was good. Those, therefore, who were curious and rude enough to stare at her were probably disappointed to find that she ate like "any Christom man."

"How do you think the Armours will receive her?" said Lambert to Mrs. Townley, of whose

29

judgment on short acquaintance he had come to
entertain a high opinion.

Mrs. Townley had a pretty way of putting
her head to one side and speaking very piquantly.
She had had it as a girl ; she had not lost it as
a woman, any more than she had lost a soft
little spontaneous laugh which was one of her
unusual charms — for few women can laugh
audibly with effect. She laughed very softly
now, and, her sense of humour supervening for
the moment, she said—

" Really, you have asked me a conundrum.
I fancy I see Mrs. Armour's face when she gets
the news,—at the breakfast-table, of course,—
and gives a little shriek, and says, 'General!
oh, General!' But it is all very shocking, you
know," she added, in a lower voice. "Still, I
think they will receive her and do the best they
can for her ; because, you see, there she is,
married hard and fast. She bears the Armour
name, and is likely to make them all very unhappy indeed if she determines to retaliate
upon them for any neglect."

" Yes. But how to retaliate, Mrs. Townley ? "
Lambert had not a suggestive mind.

" Well, for instance, suppose they sent her
away into seclusion, — with Frank's consent,
another serious question,—and she should take
the notion to fly her retirement, and appear

inopportunely at some social function clothed as she is now! I fancy her blanket would be a wet one in such a case—if you will pardon the little joke."

Lambert sighed. "Poor Frank! poor devil!" he said, almost beneath his breath.

"And wherefore poor Frank? Do you think he or the Armours of Greyhope are the only ones at stake in this? What about this poor girl? Just think why he married her,—if our suspicions are right, — and then imagine her feelings when she wakes to the truth over there, as some time she is sure to do!"

Then Lambert began to see the matter in a different light, and his sympathy for Francis Armour grew less as his pity for the girl increased. In fact, the day before they got to Liverpool he swore at Armour more than once, and was anxious concerning the reception of the heathen wife by her white relatives.

Had he been present at a certain scene at Greyhope a day or two before, he would have been still more anxious. It was the custom, at breakfast, for Mrs. Armour to open her husband's letters and read them while he was engaged with his newspaper, and hand to him afterwards those that were important. This morning Marion noticed a letter from Frank amongst the pile, and, without a word, pounced upon it. She was

31

curious—as any woman would be—to see how he took Miss Sherwood's action. Her father was deep in his paper at the time. Her mother was reading other letters. Marion read the first few lines with a feeling of almost painful wonder, the words were so curious, cynical, and cold.

Richard sat opposite her. He also was engaged with his paper, but, chancing to glance up, he saw that she was becoming very pale, and that the letter trembled in her fingers. Being a little short-sighted, he was not near enough to see the handwriting. He did not speak yet. He watched. Presently, seeing her grow more excited, he touched her foot under the table. She looked up, and caught his eye. She gasped slightly. She gave him a warning look, and turned away from her mother. Then she went on reading to the bitter end. Presently a little cry escaped her against her will. At that her mother looked up, but she only saw her daughter's back, as she rose hurriedly from the table, saying that she would return in a moment. Mrs. Armour, however, had been startled. She knew that Marion had been reading a letter, and, with a mother's instinct, her thoughts were instantly on Frank. She spoke quickly, almost sharply—

" Marion, come here."

Richard had risen. He came round the table,

32

and, as the girl obeyed her mother, took the letter from her fingers and hastily glanced over it. Mrs. Armour came forward and took her daughter's arm. "Marion," she said, "there is something wrong—with Frank. What is it?"

General Armour was now looking up at them all, curiously, questioningly, through his glasses, his paper laid down, his hands resting on the table.

Marion could not answer. She was sick with regret, vexation, and shame; at the first flush death—for Frank—had been preferable to this. She had a considerable store of vanity; she was not very philosophical. Besides, she was not married; and what Captain Vidall, her devoted admirer and possible husband, would think of this heathenish alliance was not a cheerful thought to her. She choked down a sob, and waved her hand towards Richard to answer for her. He was pale too, but cool. He understood the case instantly; he made up his mind instantly also as to what ought to be—must be—done.

"Well, mother," he said, "it is about Frank. But he is all right; that is, he is alive and well —in body. But he has arranged a hateful little embarrassment for us—he is married."

"Married?" said his mother faintly. "Oh, poor Lady Agnes!"

C        33

Marion sniffed a little viciously at this.

"Married? Married?" said his father. "Well, what about it? eh? what about it?"

The mother wrung her hands. "Oh, I know it is something dreadful—dreadful! He has married some horrible wild person, or something."

Richard, miserable as he was, remained calm. "Well," said he, "I don't know about her being horrible; Frank is silent on that point; but she is wild enough—a wild Indian, in fact!"

"Indian? Indian? Good God, a red nigger!" cried General Armour harshly, starting to his feet.

"An Indian? a wild Indian?" Mrs. Armour whispered faintly, as she dropped into a chair.

"And she'll be here in two or three days!" fluttered Marion hysterically.

Meanwhile Richard had hastily picked up the *Times*. "She is due here the day after to-morrow," he said deliberately. "Frank is as decisive as he is rash. Well, it's a melancholy tit-for-tat."

"What do you mean by tit-for-tat?" cried his father angrily.

"Oh, I mean that—that we tried to hasten Julia's marriage—with the other fellow, and he is giving us one in return; and you will all agree that it's a pretty permanent one."

The old soldier recovered himself, and was beside his wife in an instant. He took her hand. "Don't fret about it, wife," he said; "it's an ugly business, but we must put up with it. The boy was out of his head. We are old now, my dear, but there was a time when we should have resented such a thing as much as Frank,—though not in the same fashion, perhaps,—not in the same fashion!" The old man pressed his lips hard to keep down his emotion.

"Oh, how could he? how could he?" said his mother: " we meant everything for the best."

"It is always dangerous business meddling with lovers' affairs," rejoined Richard. "Lovers take themselves very seriously indeed, and— well, here the thing is! Now, who will go and fetch her from Liverpool? I should say that both my father and my mother ought to go."

Thus Richard took it for granted that they would receive Frank's Indian wife into their home. He intended that, so far as he was concerned, there should be no doubt upon the question from the beginning.

"Never! she shall never come here!" said Marion, with flashing eyes ;—" a common squaw, with greasy hair, and blankets, and big mouth, and black teeth, who eats with her fingers and grunts! If she does, if she is brought to Grey-

35

hope, I will never show my face in the world again. Frank married the animal : why does he ship her home to us? Why didn't he come with her? Why does he not take her to a home of his own? Why should he send her here, to turn our house into a menagerie?"

Marion drew her skirt back, as if the common squaw, with her blankets and grease, was at that moment near her.

"Well, you see," continued Richard, "that is just it. As I said, Frank arranged this little complication with a trifling amount of malice. No doubt he didn't come with her because he wished to test the family loyalty and hospitality ; but a postscript to this letter says that his solicitor has instructions to meet his wife at Liverpool and bring her on here in case we fail to show her proper courtesy."

General Armour here spoke. " He has carried the war of retaliation very far indeed, but men do mad things when their blood is up, as I have seen often. That doesn't alter our clear duty in the matter. If the woman were bad, or shameful, it would be a different thing ; if"—

Marion interrupted: "She has ridden bareback across the continent like a jockey,—like a common jockey,—and she wears a blanket, and she doesn't know a word of English, and she will sit on the floor ! "

"Well," said her father, "all these things are not sins, and she must be taught better."

"Joseph, how can you?" said Mrs. Armour indignantly. "She cannot, she shall not come here. Think of Marion! think of our position!"

She hid her troubled, tear-stained face behind her handkerchief. At the same time she grasped her husband's hand. She knew that he was right. She honoured him in her heart for the position he had taken, but she could not resist the natural impulse of a woman where her taste and convention were shocked.

The old man was very pale, but there was no mistaking his determination. He had been more indignant than any of them at first, but he had an unusual sense of justice when he got face to face with it, as Richard had here helped him to do. "We do not know that the woman has done any wrong," he said. "As for our name and position, they, thank God! are where a mad marriage cannot unseat them. We have had much prosperity in the world, my wife; we have had neither death nor dishonour; we"—

"If this isn't dishonour, father, what is?" Marion flashed out.

He answered calmly. "My daughter, it is a great misfortune, it will probably be a lifelong trial, but it is not necessarily dishonour."

"You never can make a scandal less by trying

37

to hide it," said Richard, backing up his father. "It is all pretty awkward, but I daresay we shall get some amusement out of it in the end."

" Richard," said his mother through her tears, "you are flippant and unkind !"

"Indeed, mother," was his reply, " I never was more serious in my life. When I spoke of amusement, I meant comedy merely, not fun,— the thing that looks like tragedy and has a happy ending. That is what I mean, mother, nothing more."

"You are always so very deep, Richard," remarked Marion ironically, " and care so very little how the rest of us feel about things. You have no family pride. If you had married a squaw, we shouldn't have been surprised. You could have camped in the grounds with your wild woman, and never have been missed—by the world," she hastened to add, for she saw a sudden pain in his face.

He turned from them all a little wearily, and limped over to the window. He stood looking out into the limes where he and Frank had played when boys. He put his finger up, his unhandsome finger, and caught away some moisture from his eyes. He did not dare to let them see his face, nor yet to speak. Marion had cut deeper than she knew, and he would carry the wound for many a day before it healed.

But his sister felt instantly how cruel she had
been, as she saw him limp away, and caught
sight of the bowed shoulders and the prema-
turely grey hair. Her heart smote her. She ran
over, and impulsively put her hands on his
shoulder. "Oh, Dick," she said, "forgive me,
Dick! I didn't mean it. I was angry and
foolish and hateful."

He took one of her hands as it rested on his
shoulder, she standing partly behind him, and
raised it to his lips, but he did not turn to her ;
he could not.

"It is all right—all right," he said ; "it doesn't
make any difference. Let us think of Frank
and what we have got to do. Let us stand
together, Marion ; that is best."

But her tears were dropping on his shoulder,
as her forehead rested on her hand. He knew
now that, whatever Frank's wife was, she would
not have an absolute enemy here; for when
Marion cried her heart was soft. She was clay
in the hands of the potter whom we call Mercy
—more often a stranger to the hearts of women
than of men. At the other side of the room
also the father and mother, tearless now, watched
these two ; and the mother saw her duty better
and with less rebelliousness. She had felt it
from the first, but she could not bring her
mind to do it. They held each other's hands

in silence. Presently General Armour said, "Richard, your mother and I will go to Liverpool to meet our son's wife."

Marion shuddered a little, and her hands closed on Richard's shoulder, but she said nothing

# CHAPTER III

## OUT OF THE NORTH

IT was a beautiful day—which was so much in favour of Mrs. Frank Armour in relation to her husband's people. General Armour and his wife had come down from London by the latest train possible, that their suspense at Liverpool might be short. They said little to each other, but when they did speak it was of things very different from the skeleton which they expected to put into the family cupboard presently. Each was trying to spare the other. It was very touching. They naturally looked upon the matter in its most unpromising light, because an Indian was an Indian, and this unknown savage from Fort Charles was in violent contrast to such desirable persons as Lady Agnes Martling. Not that the Armours were zealous for mere money and title, but the thing itself was altogether *à propos*, as Mrs. Armour had more naïvely than correctly put it. The general, whose knowledge of character and the circumstances of life was considerable, had worked out the thing with much accuracy. He had declared to Richard, in their quiet talk upon the subject, that Frank must have been anything but sober when he did it. He had previously called it a policy of retaliation ; so that now he was very near the truth. When they arrived at the dock at Liverpool, the *Aphrodite* was just making into the harbour.

" Egad," said General Armour to himself, " Sebastopol was easier than this ; for fighting I know, and being peppered I know, by Jews, Greeks, infidels, and heretics ; but to take a savage to my arms and do for her what her godfathers and godmothers never did, is worse than the devil's dance at Delhi."

What Mrs. Armour, who was not quite so definite as her husband, thought, it would be hard to tell ; but probably grief for, and indignation at, her son, were uppermost in her mind. She had quite determined upon her course. None could better carry that high, neutral look of social superiority than she.

Please Heaven, she said to herself, no one should see that her equanimity was shaken. They had brought one servant with them, who had been gravely and yet conventionally informed that his young master's wife, an Indian

42

chieftainess, was expected. There are few family troubles but find their way to servants' hall with an uncomfortable speed ; for, whether or not stone walls have ears, certainly men-servants and maid-servants have eyes that serve for ears, and ears that do more than their bounden duty. Boulter, the footman, knew his business. When informed of the coming of Mrs. Francis Armour, the Indian chieftainess, his face was absolutely expressionless; his "Yessir" was as mechanical as usual. On the dock he was marble—indifferent. When the passengers began to land, he showed no excite-ment. He was decorously alert. When the crucial moment came, he was imperturbable. Boulter was an excellent servant. So said Edward Lambert to himself after the event ; so, likewise, said Mrs. Townley to herself when the thing was over; so declared General Armour many a time after, and once very emphatically, just before he raised Boulter's wages.

As the boat neared Liverpool, Lambert and Mrs. Townley grew nervous. The truth re-garding the Indian wife had become known among the passengers, and most were very curious—some in a well-bred fashion, some intrusively, vulgarly. Mackenzie, Lali's com-panion, like Boulter, was expressionless in face. She had her duty to do, paid for liberally, and

she would do it. Lali might have had a more
presentable and dignified attendant, but not
one more worthy. It was noticeable that the
captain of the ship and all the officers had been
markedly courteous to Mrs. Armour throughout
the voyage, but, to their credit, not ostentatiously
so. When the vessel was brought to anchor
and the passengers were being put upon the
tender, the captain came and made his respectful
adieus, as though Lali were a lady of title in
her own right, and not an Indian girl married
to a man acting under the influence of brandy
and malice. General Armour and Mrs. Armour
were always grateful to Lambert and Mrs.
Townley for the part they played in this
desperate little comedy. They stood still and
watchful as the passengers came ashore one by
one. They saw that they were the centre of
unusual interest, but General Armour was used
to bearing himself with a grim kind of indifference in public, and his wife was calm, and so
somewhat disappointed those who probably
expected the old officer and his wife to be
distressed. Frank Armour's solicitor was also
there, but, with good taste, he held aloof. The
two needed all their courage, however, when
they saw a figure in buckskin and blanket step
upon the deck, attended by a very ordinary,
austere, and shabbily-dressed Scotswoman. But

44

immediately behind them were Edward Lambert and Mrs. Townley, and these, with their simple tact, naturalness, and freedom from any sort of embarrassment, acted as foils, and relieved the situation.

General Armour advanced, hat in hand. "You are my son's wife?" he said courteously to this being in a blanket.

She looked up and shook her head slightly, for she did not quite understand; but she recognised his likeness to her husband, and presently she smiled up musingly. Mackenzie repeated to her what General Armour had said. She nodded now, a flash of pleasure lighting up her face, and she slid out her beautiful hand to him. The general took it and pressed it mechanically, his lips twitching slightly. He pressed it far harder than he meant, for his feelings were at tension. She winced slightly, and involuntarily thrust out her other hand, as if to relieve his pressure. As she did so the blanket fell away from her head and shoulders. Lambert, with excellent intuition, caught it, and threw it across his arm. Then, quickly, and without embarrassment, he and Mrs. Townley greeted General Armour, who returned the greetings gravely, but in a singular, confidential tone, which showed his gratitude. Then he raised his hat again to Lali, and said, "Come and

45

let me introduce you — to your husband's mother."

The falling back of that blanket had saved the situation ; for when the girl stood without it in her buckskin garments there was a dignity in her bearing which carried off the bizarre event. There was timidity in her face, and yet a kind of pride too, though she was only a savage. The case, even at this critical moment, did not seem quite hopeless. When they came to Mrs. Armour, Lali shrank away timidly from the look in the mother's eyes, and, shivering slightly, looked round for her blanket. But Lambert had deftly passed it on to the footman. Presently Mrs. Armour took both the girl's hands in hers (perhaps she did it because the eyes of the public were on her, but that is neither here nor there—she did it), and kissed her on the cheek. Then they moved away to a closed carriage.

And that was the second act in Frank Armour's comedy of errors.

# CHAPTER IV

## IN THE NAME OF THE FAMILY

THE journey from Liverpool to Greyhope was passed in comparative silence. The Armours had a compartment to themselves, and they made the Indian girl as comfortable as possible without self-consciousness, without any artificial politeness. So far, what they had done was a matter of duty, not of will ; but they had done their duty naturally all their lives, and it was natural to them now. They had no personal feelings towards the girl one way or another, as yet. It was trying to them that people stared into the compartment at different stations. It presently dawned upon General Armour that it might also be trying to their charge. Neither he nor his wife had taken into account the possibility of the girl having feelings to be hurt. But he had noticed Lali shrink visibly and flush slightly when some one stared harder than usual, and this troubled him. It opened up a possi-

47

bility. He began indefinitely to see that they were not the only factors in the equation. He was probably a little vexed that he had not seen it before ; for he wished to be a just man. He was wont to quote with more or less austerity —chiefly the result of his professional life— this :

For justice, all place a temple, and all season summer.

And, man of war as he was, he had another saying which was much in his mouth; and he lived up to it with considerable sincerity—

Still in thy right hand carry gentle peace,
To silence envious tongues.

He whispered to his wife. It would have been hard to tell from her look what she thought of the matter, but presently she changed seats with her husband, that he might, by holding his newspaper at a certain angle, shield the girl from intrusive gazers.

At every station the same scene was enacted. And inquisitive people must have been surprised to see how monotonously ordinary was the manner of the three white people in the compartment. Suddenly, at a station near London, General Armour gave a start, and used a strong expression under his breath. Glancing at the " Marriage " column, he saw a notice to the

48

effect that on a certain day of a certain month, Francis Gilbert, the son of General Joseph Armour, C.B., of Greyhope, Hertfordshire, and Cavendish Square, was married to Lali, the daughter of Eye-of-the-Moon, chief of the Bloods, at her father's lodge in the Saskatchewan Valley. This had been inserted by Frank Armour's solicitor, according to his instructions, on the day that the *Aphrodite* was due at Liverpool. General Armour did not at first intend to show this to his wife, but on second thought he did, because he knew she would eventually come to know of it, and also because she saw that something had moved him. She silently reached out her hand for the paper. He handed it to her, pointing to the notice.

Mrs. Armour was unhappy, but her self-possession was admirable, and she said nothing. She turned her face to the window, and sat for a long time looking out. She did not turn to the others, for her eyes were full of tears, and she did not dare to wipe them away, nor yet to let them be seen. She let them dry there. She was thinking of her son, her favourite son, for whom she had been so ambitious, and for whom, so far as she could, and retain her self-respect, she had delicately intrigued, that he might happily and befittingly marry. She knew that in the matter of his engagement she had not

D      49

done what was best for him, but how could she have guessed that this would be the result? She also was sure that when the first flush of his anger and disappointment had passed, and he came to view this thing with cooler mind, he would repent deeply—for a whole lifetime. She was convinced that he had not married this savage for anything which could make marriage endurable. Under the weight of the thought she was likely to forget that the young alien wife might have lost terribly in the event also.

The arrival at Euston and the departure from St. Pancras were rather painful all round, for, though there was no waiting at either place, the appearance of an Indian girl in native costume was uncommon enough, even in cosmopolitan London, to draw much attention. Besides, the placards of the evening papers were blazoned with such announcements as this—

A RED INDIAN GIRL
MARRIED INTO
AN ENGLISH COUNTY FAMILY.

Some one had telegraphed particulars—distorted particulars—over from Liverpool, and all the evening sheets had their portion of extravagance and sensation. General Armour became a little more erect and austere as he caught sight of these placards, and Mrs. Armour groaned inwardly; but their faces were inscrutable, and they quietly conducted their charge, *minus* her blanket, to the train which was to take them to St. Albans, and were soon wheeling homeward.

At Euston they parted with Lambert and Mrs. Townley, who quite simply and conventionally bade good-bye to them and their Indian daughter-in-law. Lali had grown to like Mrs. Townley, and when they parted she spoke a few words quickly in her own tongue, and then immediately was confused, because she remembered that she could not be understood. But presently she said in halting English that the face of her white friend was good, and she hoped that she would come one time and sit beside her in her wigwam, for she would be sad till her husband travelled to her.

Mrs. Townley made some polite reply in simple English, pressed the girl's hand sympathetically, and hurried away. Before she parted from Mr. Lambert, however, she said, with a pretty touch of cynicism, "I think I see Marion Armour listening to her sister-in-law issue invitations to her wigwam. I am afraid I should be rather depressed myself if I had to be sisterly to a wigwam lady."

"But I say, Mrs. Townley," rejoined Lambert seriously, as he loitered at the steps of her

51

carriage, "I shouldn't be surprised if my lady
Wigwam—a rather apt and striking title, by the
way—turned out better than we think. She
carried herself rippingly without the blanket,
and I never saw a more beautiful hand in my
life—but one," he added, as his fingers at that
moment closed on hers, and held them tightly,
in spite of the indignant little effort at with-
drawal. "She may yet be able to give them
all points in dignity and that kind of thing, and
pay Master Frank back in his own coin. I do
not see, after all, that he is the martyr."

Lambert's voice got softer, for he still held
Mrs. Townley's fingers,—the footman not having
the matter in his eye,—and then he spoke still
more seriously on sentimental affairs of his own,
in which he evidently hoped she would take
some interest. Indeed, it is hard to tell how far
the case might have been pushed if she had not
suddenly looked a little forbidding and imperious.
For even people of no notable height, with soft
features, dark brown eyes, and a delightful little
laugh, may appear rather regal at times. Lambert did not quite understand why she should
take this attitude. If he had been as keen
regarding his own affairs of the affections as in
the case of Frank Armour and his Indian bride,
he had known that every woman has in her
mind the occasion when she should and when

she should not be wooed, and nothing disappoints her more than a declaration at a time which is not *her* time. If it does not fall out as she wishes it, retrospect, a dear thing to a woman, is spoiled. Many a man has been sent to the right-about because he has ventured his proposal at the wrong time. What would have occurred to Lambert it is hard to tell ; but he saw that something was wrong, and stopped in time.

When General Armour and his party reached Greyhope it was late in the evening. The girl seemed tired and confused by the events of the day, and did as she was directed indifferently, limply. But when they entered the gates of Greyhope and travelled up the long avenue of limes, she looked round her somewhat eagerly, and drew a long sigh, maybe of relief or pleasure. She presently stretched out a hand almost caressingly to the thick trees and the grass, and said aloud, "Oh, the beautiful trees and the long grass!" There was a whirr of birds' wings among the branches, and then, presently, there rose from a distance the sweet, gurgling whistle of the nightingale. A smile as of reminiscence crossed her face. Then she said, as if to herself, "It is the same. I shall not die. I hear the birds' wings, and one is singing. It is pleasant to sleep in the long grass when

53

the nights are summer, and to hang your cradle in the trees."

She had asked for her own blanket, refusing a rug, when they left St. Albans, and it had been given to her. She drew it about her now with a feeling of comfort, and seemed to lose the horrible sense of strangeness which had almost convulsed her when she ·was put into the carriage at the railway station. Her reserve had hidden much of what she really felt; but the drive through the limes had shown General Armour and his wife that they had to do with a nature having capacities for sensitive feeling; which, it is sometimes thought, is only the prerogative of certain well-bred civilisations.

But it was impossible that they should yet, or for many a day, feel any sense of kinship with this aboriginal girl. Presently the carriage drew up to the doorway, which was instantly open to them. A broad belt of light streamed out upon the stone steps. Far back in the hall stood Marion, one hand upon the balustrade of the staircase, the other tightly held at her side, as if to nerve herself for the meeting. The eyes of the Indian girl pierced the light, and, as if by a strange instinct, found those of Marion, even before she left the carriage. Lali felt vaguely that here was her possible enemy. As she stepped out of the carriage, General Armour's

54

hand under her elbow to assist her, she drew her blanket something more closely about her, and so proceeded up the steps. The composure of the servants was, in the circumstances, remarkable. It needed to have been, for the courage displayed by Lali's two new guardians during the day almost faltered at the threshold of their own home. Any sign of surprise or amusement on the part of the domestics would have given them some painful moments subsequently. But all was perfectly decorous. Marion still stood motionless, almost dazed. The group advanced into the hall, and there paused, as if waiting for her.

At that moment Richard came out of the study at her right hand, took her arm, and said quietly, "Come along, Marion; let us be as brave as our father and mother."

She gave a hard little gasp and seemed to awake as from a dream. She quickly glided forward ahead of him, kissed her mother and father almost abruptly, then turned to the young wife with a scrutinising eye.

" Marion," said her father, " this is your sister.'

Marion stood hesitating, confused.

" Marion dear," repeated her mother ceremoniously, "this is your brother's wife.—Lali, this is your husband's sister, Marion."

Mackenzie translated the words swiftly to the

55

girl, and her eyes flashed wide. Then in a low voice she said in English, "Yes, Marion, *How !*"

It is probable that neither Marion nor any one present knew quite the meaning of *How*, save Richard, and he could not suppress a smile, it sounded so absurd and aboriginal. But at this exclamation Marion once more came to herself. She could not possibly go so far as her mother did at the dock and kiss this savage, but, with a rather sudden grasp of the hand, she said, a little hysterically,—for her brain was going round like a wheel,—" Wo-won't you let me take your blanket?" and forthwith laid hold of it with tremulous politeness.

The question sounded, for the instant, so ludicrous to Richard that, in spite of the distressing situation, he had to choke back a laugh. Years afterwards, if he wished for any momentary revenge upon Marion (and he had a keen sense of wordy retaliation), he simply said, "Wo-won't you let me take your blanket?"

Of course the Indian girl did not understand, but she submitted to the removal of this uncommon mantle, and stood forth a less trying sight to Marion's eyes; for, as we said before, her buckskin costume set off softly the good outlines of her form.

The Indian girl's eyes wandered from Marion

56

to Richard. They wandered from anxiety, doubt, and a bitter kind of reserve, to cordiality, sympathy, and a grave kind of humour. Instantly the girl knew that she had in eccentric Richard Armour a frank friend. Unlike as he was to his brother, there was still in their eyes the same friendliness and humanity. That is, it was the same look that Frank carried when he first came to her father's lodge.

Richard held out his hand with a cordial little laugh and said, " Ah, ah, very glad, very glad ! Just in time for supper. Come along. How is Frank, eh ? how is Frank ? Just so ; just so. Pleasant journey, I suppose ? " He shook her hand warmly three or four times, and, as he held it, placed his left hand over it and patted it patriarchally, as was his custom with all the children and all the old ladies that he knew.

" Richard," said his mother, in a studiously neutral voice, "you might see about the wine."

Then Richard appeared to recover himself, and did as he was requested, but not until his brother's wife had said to him in English, as they courteously drew her towards the staircase, " Oh, my brother, Richard, *How !* "

But the first strain and suspense were now over for the family, and it is probable that never had they felt such relief as when they sat down behind closed doors in their own rooms for a short respite, while the Indian girl was closeted alone with Mackenzie and a trusted maid, in what she called her wigwam.

# CHAPTER V

IT is just as well, perhaps, that the matter had become notorious. Otherwise the Armours had lived in that unpleasant condition of being constantly "discovered." It was simply a case of aiming at absolute secresy, which had been frustrated by Frank himself, or bold and unembarrassed acknowledgment and an attempt to carry things off with a high hand. The latter course was the only one possible. It had originally been Richard's idea, appropriated by General Armour, and accepted by Mrs. Armour and Marion with what grace was possible. The publication of the event prepared their friends, and precluded the necessity for reserve. What the friends did not know was whether they ought or ought not to commiserate the Armours. It was a difficult position. A death, an accident, a lost reputation, would have been easy to them ; concerning these there could be no doubt. But an Indian daughter-in-law, a person in moccasins, was scarcely a thing to be congratulated upon; and yet sympathy and consolation might be much misplaced; no one could tell how the Armours would take it. For even their closest acquaintances knew what kind of delicate hauteur was possible to them. Even the "'centric" Richard, who visited the cottages of the poor, carrying soup and luxuries of many kinds, accompanying them with the most wholesome advice a single man ever gave to families and the heads of families, whose laugh was so cheery and spontaneous, — and face so uncommonly grave and sad at times, — had a faculty for manner. With astonishing suddenness he could raise insurmountable barriers; and people, not of his order, who occasionally presumed on his simplicity of life and habits, found themselves put distinctly ill at ease by a quiet, curious look in his eye. No man was ever more the recluse and at the same time the man of the world. He had had his bitter little comedy of life, but it was different from that of his brother Frank. It was buried very deep; not one of his family knew of it: Edward Lambert, and one or two others who had good reason never to speak of it, were the only persons possessing his secret.

But all England knew of Frank's *mésalliance*.

And the question was, What would people do ? They very properly did nothing at first. They waited to see how the Armours would act: they did not congratulate ; they did not console ; that was left to those papers which chanced to resent General Armour's politics, and those others which were emotional and sensational on every subject—particularly so where women were concerned.

It was the beginning of the season, but the Armours had decided that they would not go to town. That is, the general and his wife were not going. They felt that they ought to be at Greyhope with their daughter-in-law—which was to their credit. Regarding Marion they had nothing to say. Mrs. Armour inclined to her going to town for the season, to visit Mrs. Townley, who had thoughtfully written to her, saying that she was very lonely, and begging Mrs. Armour to let her come, if she would. She said that of course Marion would see much of her people in town just the same. Mrs. Townley was a very clever and tactful woman. She guessed that General Armour and his wife were not likely to come to town, but that must not appear, and the invitation should be on a different basis—as it was.

It is probable that Marion saw through the delicate plot, but that did not make her like

61

Mrs. Townley less. These little pieces of art make life possible, these tender fictions!

Marion was, however, not in good humour; she was nervous and a little petulant. She had a high-strung temperament, a sensitive perception of the fitness of things, and a horror of what was *gauche;* and she would, in brief, make a rather austere person if the lines of life did not run in her favour. She had something of Frank's impulsiveness and temper; it would have been a great blessing to her if she had had a portion of Richard's philosophical humour also. She was at a point of tension—her mother and Richard could see that. She was anxious— though for the world she would not have had it thought so—regarding Captain Vidall. She had never cared for anybody but him; it was possible she never would. But he did not know this, and she was not absolutely sure that his evident but as yet informal love would stand this strain —which shows how people very honourable and perfect-minded in themselves may allow a large margin to other people who are presumably honourable and perfect-minded also. There was no engagement between them, and he was not bound in any way, and could, therefore, without slashing the hem of the code, retire without any apology; but they had had that unspoken understanding which most people who love each

other show even before a word of declaration
has passed their lips. If he withdrew because
of this scandal there might be some awkward
hours for Frank Armour's wife at Greyhope ;
but, more than that, there would be a very hard-
hearted young lady to play her part in the
deceitful world ; she would be as merciless as
she could be. Naturally, being young, she
exaggerated the importance of the event, and
brooded on it. It was different with her father
and mother. They were shocked and indignant
at first, but when the first scene had been faced
they began to make the best of things all round.
That is, they proceeded at once to turn the
North American Indian into a European—a
matter of no little difficulty. A governess was
discussed ; but General Armour did not like the
idea, and Richard opposed it heartily. She
must be taught English and educated and made
possible " in Christian clothing," as Mrs. Armour
put it. Of the education they almost despaired
—all save Richard ; time, instruction, vanity,
and a dressmaker might do much as to the
other.

The evening of her arrival, Lali would not,
with any urging, put on clothes of Marion's
which had been sent in to her. And the next
morning it was still the same. She came into
the breakfast-room dressed still in buckskin and

moccasins, and though the grease had been taken out of her hair it was still combed flat. Mrs. Armour had tried to influence her through Mackenzie, but to no purpose. She was placidly stubborn.

It had been unwisely told her by Mackenzie that they were Marion's clothes. They scarcely took in the fact that the girl had pride, that she was the daughter of a chief, and a chieftainess herself, and that it was far from happy to offer her Marion's clothes to wear.

Now, Richard, when he was a lad, had been on a journey to the South Seas, and had learned some of the peculiarities of the native mind, and he did not suppose that American Indians differed very much from certain well-bred Polynesians in little matters of form and good taste. When his mother told him what had occurred before Lali entered the breakfast-room, he went directly to what he believed was the cause, and advised tact with conciliation. He also pointed out that Lali was something taller than Marion, and that she might be possessed of that general trait of humanity—vanity. Mrs. Armour had not yet got used to thinking of the girl in another manner than an intrusive being of a lower order, who was there to try their patience, but also to do their bidding. She had yet to grasp the fact that, being her son's wife, she

64

must have, therefore, a position in the house, exercising a certain authority over the servants, who, to Mrs. Armour, at first seemed of superior stuff. But Richard said to her, "Mother, I fancy you don't quite grasp the position. The girl is the daughter of a chief, and the descendant of a family of chiefs, perhaps through many generations. In her own land she has been used to respect, and has been looked up to pretty generally. Her garments are, I fancy, considered very smart in the Hudson's Bay country ; and a finely decorated blanket like hers is expensive up there. You see, we have to take the thing by comparison; so please give the girl a chance."

And Mrs. Armour answered wearily, " I suppose you are right, Richard ; you generally are in the end, though why you should be I do not know, for you never see anything of the world any more, and you moon about among the cottagers. I suppose it's your native sense and the books you read."

Richard laughed softly, but there was a queer ring in the laugh, and he came over stumblingly and put his arm round his mother's shoulder. " Never mind how I get such sense as I have, mother ; I have so much time to think, it would be a wonder if I hadn't some. But I think we had better try to study her, and coax her along,

E                                          65

and not fob her off as a very inferior person, or we shall have our hands full in earnest. My opinion is, she has got that which will save her and us too—a very high spirit, which only needs opportunity to develop into a remarkable thing; and, take my word for it, mother, if we treat her as a chieftainess, or princess, or whatever she is, and not simply as a dusky person, we shall come off better and she will come off better in the long run. She is not darker than a Spaniard, anyhow."

At this point Marion entered the room, and her mother rehearsed briefly to her what their talk had been. Marion had had little sleep, and she only lifted her eyebrows at them at first. She was in little mood for conciliation. She remembered all at once that at supper the evening before her sister-in-law had said *How!* to the butler, and had eaten the mayonnaise with a dessert spoon. But presently, because she saw they waited for her to speak, she said, with a little flutter of maliciousness, "Wouldn't it be well for Richard—he has plenty of time, and we are also likely to have it now—to put us all through a course of instruction for the training of chieftainesses? And when do you think she will be ready for a drawing-room—Her Majesty Queen Victoria's, or ours?"

"Marion!" said Mrs. Armour severely; but

66

Richard came round to her, and, with his fresh, childlike humour, put his arm round her waist and added, " Marion, I'd be willing to bet (if I were in the habit of betting) my shaky old pins here against a lock of your hair that you may present her at any drawing-room—ours or Queen Victoria's—in two years, if we go at it right; and it would serve Master Frank very well if we turned her out something, after all."

Mrs. Armour said almost eagerly, " I wish it were only possible, Richard. And what you say is true, I suppose, that she is of rank in her own country, whatever value that may have!"

Richard saw his advantage. " Well, mother," he said, " a chieftainess is a chieftainess, and I don't know but to announce her as such, and "—

"And be proud of it, as it were," put in Marion, " and pose her, and make her a prize,— a Pocahontas, wasn't it ?—and go on pretending world without end!" Marion's voice was still slightly grating, but there was in it too a faint sound of hope. " Perhaps," she said to herself, " Richard is right."

At this point the door opened and Lali entered, shown in by Colvin, her newly-appointed maid, and followed by Mackenzie, and, as we said, dressed still in her heathenish garments. She had a strong sense of dignity, for she stood still and waited. Perhaps nothing could have impressed Marion more. Had Lali been sub-servient simply, an entirely passive, unintelligent creature, she would probably have tyrannised over her in a soft, persistent fashion, and despised her generally. But Mrs. Armour and Marion saw that this stranger might become very troublesome indeed, if her temper were to have play. They were aware of capacities for passion in those dark eyes, so musing yet so active in expression, which moved swiftly from one object to another and then suddenly became resolute.

Both mother and daughter came forward, and held out their hands, wishing her a pleasant good-morning, and were followed by Richard, and immediately by General Armour, who had entered soon after her. She had been keen enough to read (if a little vaguely) behind the scenes, and her mind was wakening slowly to the peculiarity of the position she occupied. The place awed her, and had broken her rest by perplexing her mind, and she sat down to the breakfast-table with a strange hunted look in her face. But opposite to her was a window opening to the ground, and beyond it were the limes and beeches and a wide perfect sward, and far away a little lake, on which swans and wild fowl fluttered. Presently, as she sat silent,

68

eating little, her eyes lifted to the window. They flashed instantly, her face lighted up with a weird kind of charm, and suddenly she got to her feet with Indian exclamations on her lips, and, as if unconscious of them all, went swiftly to the window and out of it, waving her hands up and down once or twice to the trees and the sunlight.

"What did she say?" said Mrs. Armour, rising with the others.

"She said," replied Mackenzie, as she hurried towards the window, "that they were her beautiful woods, and there were wild birds flying and swimming in the water, as in her own country."

By this time all were at the window, Richard arriving last, and the Indian girl turned on them, her body all quivering with excitement, laughed a low, birdlike laugh, and then, clapping her hands above her head, she swung round and ran like a deer towards the lake, shaking her head back as an animal does when fleeing from his pursuers. She would scarcely have been recognised as the same placid, speechless woman in a blanket who sat with folded hands day after day on the *Aphrodite*.

The watchers turned and looked at each other in wonder. Truly, their task of civilising a savage would not lack in interest. The old

69

general was better pleased, however, at this display of activity and excitement than at yesterday's taciturnity. He loved spirit, even if it had to be subdued, and he thought on the instant that he might possibly come to look upon the fair savage as an actual and not a nominal daughter‑in‑law. He had a keen appreciation of courage, and he thought he saw in her face, as she turned upon them, a look of defiance or daring, and nothing could have got at his nature quicker. If the case had not been so near to his own hearthstone he would have chuckled. As it was, he said good-humouredly that Mackenzie and Marion should go and bring her back. But Mackenzie was already at that duty. Mrs. Armour had had the presence of mind to send for Colvin ; but presently, when the general spoke, she thought it better that Marion should go, and counselled returning to breakfast and not making the matter of too much importance. This they did, Richard very reluctantly ; while Marion, rather pleased than not at the spirit shown by the strange girl, ran away over the grass towards the lake, where Lali had now stopped. There was a little bridge at one point where the lake narrowed, and Lali, evidently seeing it all at once, went towards it, and ran up on it, standing poised above the water about the middle of it. For

an instant an unpleasant possibility came into
Marion's mind : suppose the excited girl intended
suicide! She shivered as she thought of it, and
yet——! She put *that* horribly cruel and selfish
thought away from her with an indignant word
at herself. She had passed Mackenzie, and
came first to the lake. Here she slackened,
and waved her hand playfully to the girl, so
as not to frighten her ; and then with a forced
laugh came up panting on the bridge, and was
presently by Lali's side. Lali eyed her a little
furtively, but, seeing that Marion was much
inclined to be pleasant, she nodded to her, said
some Indian words hastily, and spread out her
hands towards the water. As she did so,
Marion noticed again the beauty of those hands
and the graceful character of the gesture, so
much so that she forgot the flat hair and the
unstayed body, and the rather broad feet, and
the delicate duskiness, which had so worked
upon her in imagination and in fact the evening
before. She put her hand kindly on that long
slim hand stretched out beside her, and, because
she knew not what else to speak, and because
the tongue is very perverse at times,—saying
the opposite of what is expected,—she herself
blundered out, "*How! How!* Lali."

Perhaps Lali was as much surprised at the
remark as Marion herself, and certainly very

71

much more delighted. The sound of those
familiar words, spoken by accident as they were,
opened the way to a better understanding, as
nothing else could possibly have done. Marion
was annoyed with herself, and yet amused too.
If her mind had been perfectly assured regarding
Captain Vidall, it is probable that then and
there a peculiar, a genial, comradeship would
have been formed. As it was, Marion found
this little event more endurable than she
expected. She also found that Lali, when she
laughed in pleasant acknowledgment of that
*How !* had remarkably white and regular teeth.
Indeed, Marion Armour began to discover some
estimable points in the appearance of her savage
sister-in-law. Marion remarked to herself that
Lali might be a rather striking person, if she
were dressed, as her mother said, in Christian
garments, could speak the English language
well—and was somebody else's sister-in-law.

At this point Mackenzie came breathlessly
to the bridge, and called out a little sharply to
Lali, rebuking her. In this Mackenzie made
a mistake ; for not only did Lali draw herself
up with considerable dignity, but Marion,
noticing the masterful nature of the tone,
instantly said, " Mackenzie, you must remember
that you are speaking to Mrs. Francis Armour,
and that her position in General Armour's house

is the same as mine. I hope it is not necessary to say anything more, Mackenzie."

Mackenzie flushed. She was a sensible woman, she knew that she had done wrong, and she said very promptly, "I am very sorry, miss; I was flustered, and I expect I haven't got used to speaking to—to Mrs. Armour as I'll be sure to do in the future."

As she spoke, two or three deer came trotting out of the beeches down to the lake side. If Lali was pleased and excited before, she was overwhelmed now. Her breath came in quick little gasps; she laughed; she tossed her hands; she seemed to become dizzy with delight; and presently, as if this new link with, and reminder of, her past, had moved her as one little expects a savage heart to be moved, two tears gathered in her eyes, then slid down her cheek unheeded, and dried there in the sunlight, as she still gazed at the deer. Marion, at first surprised, was now touched, as she could not have thought it possible concerning this wild creature, and her hand went out and caught Lali's gently. At this genuine act of sympathy, instinctively felt by Lali,—the stranger in a strange land, husbanded and yet a widow,—there came a flood of tears, and, dropping on her knees, she leaned against the low railing of the bridge and wept silently. So passionless was her grief it

73

seemed the more pathetic, and Marion dropped
on her knees beside her, put her arm round her
shoulder, and said, " Poor girl ! Poor girl ! "

At that Lali caught her hand, and held it
repeating after her the words, " Poor girl !
Poor girl ! "

She did not quite understand them, but
she remembered that once just ·before she
parted from her husband at the Great Lakes
he had said those very words. If the fates
had apparently given things into Frank
Armour's hands when he sacrificed this girl
to his revenge, they were evidently inclined to
play a game which would eventually defeat
his purpose, wicked as it had been in effect if
not in absolute motive. What the end of this
attempt to engraft the Indian girl upon the
strictest convention of English social life would
have been had her introduction not been at
Greyhope, where faint likenesses to her past
surrounded her, it is hard to conjecture. But,
from present appearances, it would seem that
Richard Armour was not wholly a false prophet ;
for the savage had shown herself that morning
to possess, in their crudeness, some striking
qualities of character. Given character, many
things are possible, even to those who are not
of the elect.

This was the beginning of better things

Lali seemed to the Armours not quite so impossible now. Had she been of the very common order of Indian "pure and simple," the task had resolved itself into making a common savage into a very common European. But, whatever Lali was, it was abundantly evident that she must be reckoned with at all points, and that she was more likely to become a very startling figure in the Armour household than a mere encumbrance to be blushed for, whose eternal absence were preferable to her company.

Years after that first morning Marion caught herself shuddering at the thought that came to her when she saw Lali hovering on the bridge. Whatever Marion's faults were, she had a fine dislike of anything that seemed unfair. She had not ridden to hounds for nothing. She had at heart the sportsman's instinct. It was upon this basis, indeed, that Richard appealed to her in the first trying days of Lali's life among them. To oppose your will to Marion on the basis of superior knowledge was only to turn her into a rebel ; and a very effective rebel she made ; for she had a pretty gift at the retort courteous, and she could take as much, and as well, as she gave. She rebelled at first at assisting in Lali's education, though by fits and starts she would teach her English words, and help her to form long sentences, and was, on the whole, quite patient. But Lali's real instructors were Mrs. Armour and Richard ; her best, Richard.

The first few days she made but little progress, for everything was strange to her, and things made her giddy, — the servants, the formal routine, the handsome furnishings, Marion's music, the great house, the many precise personal duties set for her, to be got through at stated times ; and Mrs. Armour's rather grand manner. But there was the relief to this, else the girl had pined terribly for her native woods and prairies ; this was the park, the deer, the lake, the hares and birds. While she sat saying over after Mrs. Armour words and phrases in English, or was being shown how she must put on and wear the clothes which a dressmaker from Regent Street had been brought to make, her eyes would wander dreamily to the trees and the lake and the grass. They soon discovered that she would pay no attention and was straightway difficult to teach if she was not placed where she could look out on the park. They had no choice, for though her resistance was never active it was nevertheless effective.

Presently she got on very swiftly with Richard. For he, with instinct worthy of a woman, turned their lessons upon her own country and Frank. This cost him something, but it had its reward. There was no more listlessness. Previously

76

Frank's name had scarcely been spoken to her. Mrs. Armour would have hours of hesitation and impotent regret before she brought herself to speak of her son to his Indian wife. Marion tried to do it a few times and failed ; the general did it with rather a forced voice and manner, because he saw that his wife was very tender upon the point. But Richard, who never knew self-consciousness, spoke freely of Frank when he spoke at all ; and it was seeing Lali's eyes brighten and her look earnestly fixed on him when he chanced to mention Frank's name, that determined him on his new method of instruction. It had its dangers, but he had calculated them all. The girl must be educated at all costs. The sooner that occurred the sooner would she see her own position and try to adapt herself to her responsibilities, and face the real state of her husband's attitude towards her.

He succeeded admirably. Striving to tell him about her past life, and ready to talk endlessly about her husband, of his prowess in the hunt, of his strength and beauty, she also strove to find English words for the purpose, and Richard supplied them with uncommon willingness. He humoured her so far as to learn many Indian words and phrases, but he was chary of his use of them, and tried hard to make her appreciative of her new life and surroundings.

He watched her waking slowly to an understanding of the life, and of all that it involved. It gave him a kind of fear, too, because she was sensitive, and there was the possible danger of her growing disheartened or desperate, and doing some mad thing in the hour that she wakened to the secret behind her marriage.

His apprehensions were not without cause. For slowly there came into Lali's mind the element of comparison. She became conscious of it one day when some neighbouring people called at Greyhope. Mrs. Armour, in her sense of duty, which she had rigidly set before her, introduced Lali into the drawing-room. The visitors veiled their curiosity and said some pleasant casual things to the young wife, but she saw the half-curious, half-furtive glances, she caught a sidelong glance and smile, and when they were gone she took to looking at herself in a mirror, a thing she could scarcely be persuaded to do before. She saw the difference between her carriage and theirs, her manner of wearing her clothes and theirs, her complexion and theirs. She exaggerated the difference. She brooded on it. Now she sat downcast and timid, and hunted in face, as on the first evening she came ; now she appeared restless and excited.

If Mrs. Armour was not exactly sympathetic

with her, she was quiet and forbearing, and General Armour, like Richard, tried to draw her out—but not on the same subjects. He dwelt upon what she did ; the walks she took in the park, those hours in the afternoon when, with Mackenzie or Colvin, she vanished into the beeches, making friends with the birds and deer and swans. But most of all she loved to go to the stables. She was, however, asked not to go unless Richard or General Armour was with her. She loved horses, and these were a wonder to her. She had never known any but the wild, ungroomed Indian pony, on which she had ridden in every fashion and over every kind of country. Mrs. Armour sent for a riding-master, and had riding-costumes made for her. It was intended that she should ride every day as soon as she seemed sufficiently presentable This did not appear so very far off, for she improved daily in appearance. Her hair was growing finer, and was made up in the modest prevailing fashion ; her skin, no longer exposed to an inclement climate, and subject to the utmost care, was smoother and fairer ; her feet, encased in fine, well-made boots, looked much smaller ; her waist was shaped to fashion, and she was very straight and lissom. So many things she did jarred on her relatives, that they were not fully aware of the great

79

improvement in her appearance. Even Richard admitted her trying at times.

Marion went up to town to stay with Mrs. Townley, and there had to face a good deal of curiosity. People looked at her sometimes as if it was she and not Lali that was an Indian. But she carried things off bravely enough, and answered those kind inquiries, which one's friends make when we are in embarrassing situations, with answers so calm and pleasant that people did not know what to think.

"Yes," she said, in reply to Lady Balwood, "her sister-in-law might be in town later in the year, perhaps before the season was over : she could not tell. She was tired after her long voyage, and she preferred the quiet of Grey-hope ; she was fond of riding and country-life ; but still she would come to town for a time." And so on.

"Ah, dear me, how charming ! And doesn't she resent her husband's absence—during the honeymoon ? or did the honeymoon occur before she came over to England ? " And Lady Bal-wood tried to say it all playfully, and certainly said it something loudly. She had daughters.

But Marion was perfectly prepared. Her face did not change expression. " Yes, they had had their honeymoon on the prairies, Frank was so fascinated with the life and the people.

He had not come home at once, because he was
making she did not know how great a fortune
over there in investments, and so Mrs. Armour
came on before him, and, of course, as soon as
he could get away from his business, he would
follow his wife."

And though Marion smiled, her heart was
very hot, and she could have slain Lady
Balwood in her tracks. Lady Balwood then
nodded a little patronisingly, and babbled that
" she hoped so much to see Mrs. Francis Armour.
She must be so very interesting, the papers said
so much about her."

Now, while this conversation was going on,
some one stood not far behind Marion, who
seemed much interested in her and what she
said. But Marion did not see this person. She
was startled presently, however, to hear a strong
voice say softly over her shoulder, " What a
charming woman Lady Balwood is ! And so
ingenuous ! "

She was grateful, tremulous, proud. Why
had he—Captain Vidall—kept out of the way
all these weeks, just when she needed him most,
just when he should have played the part of a
man ? Then she was feeling twinges at the
heart, too. She had seen Lady Agnes Martling
that afternoon, and had noticed how the news
had worn on her. She felt how much better

F                     81

it had been had Frank come quietly home and married her, instead of doing the wild, scandalous thing that was making so many heart-burnings. A few minutes ago she had longed for a chance to say something delicately acid to Lady Haldwell, once Julia Sherwood, who was there. Now there was a chance to give her bitter spirit tongue. She was glad— she dared not think how glad—to hear that voice again ; but she was angry too, and he should suffer for it,—the more so because she recognised in the tone, and afterwards in his face, that he was still absorbingly interested in her. There was a little burst of thanksgiving in her heart, and then she prepared a very notable commination service in her mind.

This meeting had been deftly arranged by Mrs. Townley, with the help of Edward Lambert, who now held her fingers with a kind of vanity of possession whenever he bade her good-bye or met her. Captain Vidall had, in fact, been out of the country, had only been back a week, and had only heard of Frank Armour's *mésalliance* from Lambert at an At Home forty-eight hours before. Mrs. Townley guessed what was really at the bottom of Marion's occasional bitterness, and, piecing together many little things dropped casually by her friend, had come to the conclusion that the happiness of two people was at stake.

When Marion shook hands with Captain Vidall she had herself exceedingly well under control. She looked at him in slight surprise, and casually remarked that they had not chanced to meet lately in the run of small-and-earlies. She appeared to be unconscious that he had been out of the country, and also that she had been till very recently indeed at Grey-hope. He hastened to assure her that he had been away, and to lay siege to this unexpected barrier. He knew all about Frank's affair, and, though it troubled him, he did not see why it should make any difference in his regard for Frank's sister. Fastidious as he was in all things, he was fastidiously deferential. Not an exquisite, he had all that vanity as to appearance so usual with the military man; himself of the most perfect temper and sweetness of manner and conduct, the unusual disturbed him. Not possessed of a vivid imagination, he could scarcely conjure up this Indian bride at Greyhope.

But face to face with Marion Armour he saw what troubled him, and he determined that he would not meet her irony with irony, her assumed indifference with indifference. He had learned one of the most important lessons

83

of life—never to quarrel with a woman. Whoever has so far erred has been foolish indeed.
It is the worst of policy, to say nothing of its
being the worst of art; and life should never be
without art. It is absurd to be perfectly natural;
anything, anybody can be that. Well, Captain
Hume Vidall was something of an artist, more,
however, in principle than by temperament.
He refused to recognise the rather malicious
adroitness with which Marion turned his re-
marks again upon himself, twisted out of all
semblance. He was very patient. He inquired
quietly, and as if honestly interested, about
Frank, and said—because he thought it safest
as well as most reasonable—that, naturally, they
must have been surprised at his marrying a
native; but he himself had seen some such
marriages turn out very well—in Japan, India,
the South Sea Islands, and Canada. He assumed that Marion's sister-in-law was beautiful,
and then disarmed Marion by saying that he
thought of going down to Greyhope immediately, to call on General Armour and Mrs.
Armour, and wondered if she was going back
before the end of the season.

Quick as Marion was, this was said so quietly
that she did not quite see the drift of it. She
had intended staying in London to the end of
the season, not because she enjoyed it, but

because she was determined to face Frank's marriage at every quarter, and have it over, once for all, so far as herself was concerned. But now, taken slightly aback, she said, almost without thinking, that she would probably go back soon—she was not quite sure ; but certainly her father and mother would be glad to see Captain Vidall at any time.

Then, without any apparent relevancy, he asked her if Mrs. Frank Armour still wore her Indian costume. In any one else the question had seemed impertinent ; in him it had a touch of confidence, of the privilege of close friendship. Then he said, with a meditative look and a very calm, retrospective voice, that he was once very much in love with a native girl in India, and might have become permanently devoted to her, were it not for the accident of his being ordered back to England summarily.

This was a piece of news which cut two ways. In the first place it lessened the extraordinary character of Frank's marriage, and it roused in her an immediate curiosity—which a woman always feels in the past "affairs" of her lover, or possible lover. Vidall did not take pains to impress her with the fact that the matter occurred when he was almost a boy ; and it was when her earnest inquisition had drawn from him, bit by bit, the circumstances of the case, and she had forgotten many parts of her commination service and to preserve an effective neutrality in tone, that she became aware he was speaking ancient history. Then it was too late to draw back.

They had threaded their way through the crowd into the conservatory, where they were quite alone, and there, with only a little pyramid of hydrangeas between them, which she could not help but notice chimed well with the colour of her dress, he dropped his voice a little lower, and then suddenly said, his eyes hard on her, "I want your permission to go to Greyhope."

The tone drew her eyes hastily to his, and, seeing, she dropped them again. Vidall had a strong will, and, what is of more consequence, a peculiarly attractive voice. It had a vibration which made some of his words organ-like in sound. She felt the influence of it. She said a little faintly, her fingers toying with a hydrangea, "I am afraid I do not understand. There is no reason why you should not go to Greyhope without my permission."

"I cannot go without it," he persisted. "I am waiting for my commission from you."

She dropped her hand from the flower with a little impatient motion. She was tired, her head ached, she wanted to be alone. "Why are you enigmatical?" she said. Then quickly,

85

"I wish I knew what is in your mind. You play with words so."

She scarcely knew what she said. A woman who loves a man very much is not quick to take in the absolute declaration of that man's love on the instant; it is too wonderful for her. He felt his cheek flush with hers, he drew her look again to his. "Marion! Marion!" he said. That was all.

"Oh, hush! some one is coming," was her quick, throbbing reply. When they parted a half-hour later, he said to her, "Will you give me my commission to go to Greyhope?"

"Oh no, I cannot," she said very gravely; "but come to Greyhope—when I go back."

"And when will that be?" he said, smiling, yet a little ruefully too.

"Oh, ask Mrs. Townley," she replied; "she is coming also."

Marion knew what that commission to go to Greyhope meant. But she determined that he should see Lali first, before anything irrevocable was done. She still looked upon Frank's marriage as a scandal. Well, Captain Vidall should face it in all its crudeness. So, in a week or less, Marion and Mrs. Townley were in Greyhope.

Two months had gone since Lali arrived in England, and yet no letter had come to her, or

87

to any of them, from Frank. Frank's solicitor
in London had written him fully of her arrival,
and he had had a reply, with further instructions
regarding money to be placed to General
Armour's credit for the benefit of his wife.
Lali, as she became Europeanised, also awoke
to the forms and ceremonies of her new life.
She had overheard Frank's father·and mother
wondering, and fretting as they wondered, why
they had not received any word from him.
General Armour had even called him a scoundrel,
which sent Frank's mother into tears. Then
Lali had questioned Mackenzie and Colvin, for
she had increasing shrewdness, and she began
to feel her actual position. She resented General
Armour's imputation, but in her heart she began
to pine and wonder. At times, too, she was
fitful, and was not to be drawn out. But she
went on improving in personal appearance and
manner and in learning the English language.
Mrs. Townley's appearance marked a change
in her. When they met she suddenly stood still
and trembled. When Mrs. Townley came to
her and took her hand and kissed her, she
shivered, and then caught her about the shoulders
lightly, but was silent. After a little she said,
" Come—come to my wigwam, and talk with
me."

She said it with a strange little smile, for now

she recognised that the word *wigwam* was not
to be used in her new life. But Mrs. Townley
whispered, " Ask Marion to come too."

Lali hesitated, and then said, a little malici-
ously, " Marion, will you come to my wigwam ? "

Marion ran to her, caught her about the waist,
and replied gaily, " Yes, we will have a *pow-wow*
—is that right ? is *pow-wow* right ? "

The Indian girl shook her head with a pretty
vagueness, and vanished with them. General
Armour walked up and down the room briskly,
then turned on his wife and said, " Wife, it was
a brutal thing : Frank doesn't deserve to be—
the father of her child."

But Lali had moods—singular moods. She
indulged in one three days after the arrival of
Marion and Mrs. Townley. She had learned to
ride with the side-saddle, and wore her riding-
dress admirably. Nowhere did she show to
better advantage. She had taken to riding now
with General Armour on the country roads.
On this day Captain Vidall was expected, he
having written to ask that he might come.
What trouble Lali had with one of the servants
that morning was never thoroughly explained,
but certain it is, she came to have a crude
notion of why Frank Armour married her. The
servant was dismissed duly, but that was after
the *contre-temps.*

It was late afternoon. Everybody had been busy, because one or two other guests were expected besides Captain Vidall. Lali had kept to herself, sending word through Richard that she would not "be English," as she vaguely put it, that day. She had sent Mackenzie on some mission. She sat on the floor of her room, as she used to sit on the ground in her father's lodge. Her head was bowed in her hands, and her arms rested on her knees. Her body swayed to and fro. Presently all motion ceased. She became perfectly still. She looked before her as if studying something.

Her eyes immediately flashed. She rose quickly to her feet, went to her wardrobe, and took out her Indian costume and blanket, with which she could never be induced to part. Almost feverishly she took off the clothes she wore and hastily threw them from her. Then she put on the buckskin clothes in which she had journeyed to England, drew down her hair as she used to wear it, fastened round her waist a long red sash which had been given her by a governor of the Hudson's Bay Company when he had visited her father's country, threw her blanket round her shoulders, and then eyed herself in the great mirror in the room. What she saw evidently did not please her perfectly, for she stretched out her hands and looked at

90

them ; she shook her head at herself and put
her hand to her cheeks and pinched them,—
they were not so brown as they once were,—
then she thrust out her foot. She drew it back
quickly in disdain. Immediately she caught
the fashionable slippers from her feet and threw
them among the discarded garments. She
looked at herself again. Still she was not
satisfied, but she threw up her arms, as with a
sense of pleasure and freedom, and laughed at
herself. She pushed out her moccasined foot,
tapped the floor with it, nodded towards it, and
said a word or two in her own language. She
heard some one in the next room, possibly
Mackenzie. She stepped to the door leading
into the hall, opened it, went out, travelled its
length, ran down a back hallway, out into the
park, towards the stables, her blanket, as her
hair, flying behind her.

She entered the stables, made for a horse that
she had ridden much, put a bridle on him, led
him out before any one had seen her, and, catching him by the mane, suddenly threw herself on
him at a bound, and, giving him a tap with a
short whip she had caught up in the stable,
headed him for the main avenue and the open
road. Then a stableman saw her and ran after,
but he might as well have tried to follow
the wind. He forthwith proceeded to saddle

another horse. Boulter also saw her as she passed the house, and, running in, told Mrs. Armour and the general. They both ran to the window and saw dashing down the avenue—a picture out of Fenimore Cooper; a saddleless horse with a rider whose fingers merely touched the bridle, riding as on a journey of life and death.

"My God! it's Lali! She's mad! she's mad! She is striking that horse! It will bolt! It will kill her!" said the general.

Then he rushed for a horse to follow her. Mrs. Armour's hands clasped painfully. For an instant she had almost the same thought as had Marion on the first morning of Lali's coming; but that passed, and left her gazing helplessly after the horsewoman. The flying blanket had frightened the blooded horse, and he made desperate efforts to fulfil the general's predictions.

Lali soon found that she had miscalculated. She was not riding an Indian pony, but a crazed, high-strung horse. As they flew, she sitting superbly and tugging at the bridle, the party coming from the railway station entered the great gate, accompanied by Richard and Marion. In a moment they sighted this wild pair bearing down upon them with a terrible swiftness.

As Marion recognised Lali she turned pale and cried out, rising in her seat. Instinctively

Captain Vidall knew who it was, though he could not guess the cause of the singular circumstance. He saw that the horse had bolted, but also that the rider seemed entirely fearless. "Why, in Heaven's name," he said between his teeth, "does she not let go that blanket?"

At that moment Lali did let it go, and the horse dashed by them, making hard for the gate. "Turn the horses round and follow her," said Vidall to the driver. While this was doing, Marion caught sight of her father riding hard down the avenue. He passed them, and called to them to hurry on after him.

Lali had not the slightest sense of fear, but she knew that the horse had gone mad. When they passed through the gate and swerved into the road, a less practised rider would have been thrown. She sat like wax. The pace was incredible for a mile, and though General Armour rode well, he was far behind.

Suddenly a trap appeared in the road in front of them, and the driver, seeing the runaway, set his horses at right angles to the road. It served the purpose only to provide another danger. Not far from where the trap was drawn, and between it and the runaway, was a lane, which ended at a farmyard in a *cul-de-sac*. The horse swerved into it, not

93

slacking its pace, and in the fraction of a minute came to the farmyard.

But now the fever was in Lali's blood. She did not care whether she lived or died. A high hedge formed the *cul-de-sac.* When she saw the horse slacking she cut it savagely across the head twice with a whip, and drove him at the green wall. He was of too good make to refuse it, stiff as it was. He rose to it magnificently, and cleared it; but almost as he struck the ground squarely, he staggered and fell— the girl beneath him. He had burst a blood-vessel. The ground was soft and wet; the weight of the horse prevented her from getting free. She felt its hoof striking in its death-struggles, and once her shoulder was struck. Instinctively she buried her face in the mud, and her arms covered her head.

And then she knew no more.

When she came to, she was in the carriage within the gates of Greyhope, and Marion was bending over her. She suddenly tried to lift herself, but could not. Presently she saw another face — that of General Armour. It was stern, and yet his eyes were swimming as he looked at her.

"*How!*" she said to him,—"*How!*" and fainted again.

# CHAPTER VI

## THE PASSING OF THE YEARS

LALI'S recovery was not rapid. A change had come upon her. With that strange ride had gone the last strong flicker of the desire for savage life in her. She knew now the position she held towards her husband: that he had never loved her; that she was only an instrument for unworthy retaliation. So soon as she could speak after her accident, she told them that they must not write to him and tell him of it. She also made them promise that they would give him no news of her at all, save that she was well. They could not refuse to promise; they felt she had the right to demand much more than that. They had begun to care for her for herself, and when the months went by, and one day there was a hush about her room, and anxiety, and then relief, in the faces of all, they came to care for her still more for the sake of her child.

95

As the weeks passed, the fair-haired child grew more and more like his father; but if Lali thought of her husband they never knew it by anything she said, for she would not speak of him. She also made them promise that they would not write to him of the child's birth. Richard, with his sense of justice, and knowing how much the woman had been wronged, said that in all this she had done quite right; that Frank, if he had done his duty after marrying her, should have come with her. And because they all felt that Richard had been her best friend as well as their own, they called the child after him. This also was Lali's wish. Coincident with her motherhood there came to Lali a new purpose. She had not lived with the Armours without absorbing some of their fine social sense and dignity. This, added to the native instinct of pride in her, gave her a new ambition. As hour by hour her child grew dear to her, so hour by hour her husband grew away from her. She schooled herself against him. At times she thought she hated him. She felt she could never forgive him, but she would prove to him that it was she who had made the mistake of her life in marrying him; that she had been wronged, not he; and that his sin would face him with reproach and punishment one day. Richard's

96

prophecy was likely to come true: she would defeat very perfectly indeed Frank's intentions. After the child was born, so soon as she was able, she renewed her studies with Richard and Mrs. Armour. She read every morning for hours; she rode; she practised all those graceful arts of the toilet which belong to the social convention; she showed an unexpected faculty for singing, and practised it faithfully; and she begged Mrs. Armour and Marion to correct her at every point where correction seemed necessary. When the child was two years old, they all went to London, something against Lali's personal feelings, but quite in accord with what she felt her duty.

Richard was left behind at Greyhope. For the first time in eighteen months he was alone with his old quiet duties and recreations. During that time he had not neglected his pensioners,—his poor, sick, halt, and blind,—but a deeper, larger interest had come into his life in the person of Lali. During all that time she had seldom been out of his sight, never out of his influence and tutelage. His days had been full, his every hour had been given a keen, responsible interest. As if by tacit consent, every incident or development of Lali's life was influenced by his judgment and decision. He had been more to her than General Armour,

G                    97

Mrs. Armour, or Marion. Schooled as he was in all the ways of the world, he had at the same time a mind as sensitive as a woman's, an indescribable gentleness, a persuasive temperament. Since, years before, he had withdrawn from the social world and become a recluse, many of his finer qualities had gone into an indulgent seclusion. He had once loved the world and the gay life of London, but some untoward event, coupled with a radical love of retirement, had sent him into years of isolation at Greyhope.

His tutelar relations with Lali had reopened many an old spring of sensation and experience. Her shy dependency, her innocent inquisitiveness, had searched out his remotest sympathies. In teaching her he had himself been re-taught. Before she came he had been satisfied with the quiet usefulness and studious ease of his life. But in her presence something of his old youthfulness came back, some reflection of the ardent hopes of his young manhood. He did not notice the change in himself. He only knew that his life was very full. He read later at nights, he rose earlier in the morning. But, unconsciously to himself, he was undergoing a change. The more a man's sympathies and emotions are active, the less is he the philosopher. It is only when one has withdrawn from the more personal influence of the emotions that one's philosophy may be trusted. One may be interested in mankind and still be philosophical—may be, as it were, the priest and confessor to all comers. But let one be touched in some vital corner in one's nature, and the high, faultless impartiality is gone. In proportion as Richard's interest in Lali had grown, the universal quality of his sympathy had declined. Man is only man. Not that his benefactions as lord bountiful in the parish had grown perfunctory, but the calm detail of his interest was not so definite. He was the same, yet not the same.

He was not aware of any difference in himself. He did not know that he looked younger by ten years. Such is the effect of mere personal sympathy upon a man's look and bearing. When, therefore, one bright May morning, the family at Greyhope, himself excluded, was ready to start for London, he had no thought but that he would drop back into his old silent life, as it was before Lali came, and his brother's child was born. He was not conscious that he was very restless that morning; he scarcely was aware that he had got up two hours earlier than usual. At the breakfast-table he was cheerful and alert. After breakfast he amused himself in playing with the child till the carriage was

99

brought round. It was such a morning as does not come a dozen times a year in England. The sweet, moist air blew from the meadows and up through the lime trees with a warm, insinuating gladness. The lawn sloped delightfully away to the flowered embrasures of the park, and a fragrant abundance of flowers met the eye and cheered the senses. While Richard loitered on the steps with the child and its nurse, more excited than he knew, Lali came out and stood beside him. At the moment Richard was looking into the distance. He did not hear her when she came. She stood near him for a moment, and did not speak. Her eyes followed the direction of his look, and idled tenderly with the prospect before her. She did not even notice the child. The same thought was in the mind of both—with a difference. Richard was wondering how any one could choose to change the sweet dignity of that rural life for the flaring, hurried delights of London and the season. He had thought this a thousand times, and yet, though he would have been little willing to acknowledge it, his conviction was not so impregnable as it had been.

Mrs. Francis Armour was stepping from the known to the unknown. She was leaving the precincts of a life in which, socially, she had been born again. Its sweetness and benign

100

quietness had all worked upon her nature and origin to change her. In that it was an out-door life, full of freshness and open-air vigour, it was not antagonistic to her past. Upon this sympathetic basis had been imposed the conditions of a fine social decorum. The conditions must still exist. But how would it be when she was withdrawn from this peaceful activity of nature and set down among "those garish lights" in Cavendish Square and Piccadilly? She hardly knew to what she was going as yet. There had been a few social functions at Grey-hope since she had come, but that could give her, after all, but little idea of the swing and pressure of London life.

At this moment she was lingering over the scene before her. She was wondering with the naïve wonder of an awakened mind. She had intended many times of late saying to Richard all the native gratitude she felt; yet somehow she had never been able to say it. The moment of parting had come.

"What are you thinking of, Richard?" she said now.

He started and turned towards her.

"I hardly know," he answered. "My thoughts were drifting."

"Richard," she said abruptly, "I want to thank you."

"Thank me for what, Lali?" he questioned.

"To thank you, Richard, for everything—since I came, over three years ago."

He broke out into a soft little laugh, then, with his old good-natured manner, caught her hand as he did the first night she came to Greyhope, patted it in a fatherly fashion, and said—

"It is the wrong way about, Lali; I ought to be thanking you, not you me. Why, look what a stupid old fogy I was then, toddling about the place with too much time on my hands, reading a lot and forgetting everything; and here you came in, gave me something to do, made the little I know of any use, and ran a pretty gold wire down the rusty fiddle of life. If there are any speeches of gratitude to be made, they are mine, they are mine."

"Richard," she said very quietly and gravely, "I owe you more than I can ever say—in English. You have taught me to speak in your tongue enough for all the usual things of life, but one can only speak from the depths of one's heart in one's native tongue. And see," she added, with a painful little smile, "how strange it would sound if I were to tell you all I thought in the language of my people—of my people, whom I shall never see again. Richard, can you understand what it must be to have a father whom one is never likely to see again?—

whom, if one did see again, something painful would happen? We grow away from people against our will; we feel the same towards them, but they cannot feel the same towards us; for their world is in another hemisphere. We want to love them, and we love, remember, and are glad to meet them again, but they feel that we are unfamiliar, and, because we have grown different outwardly, they seem to miss some chord that used to ring. Richard, I—I"— She paused.

"Yes, Lali," he assented,—"yes, I understand you so far; but speak out."

"I am not happy," she said. "I never shall be happy. I have my child, and that is all I have. I cannot go back to the life in which I was born; I must go on as I am, a stranger among a strange people, pitied, suffered, cared for a little—and that is all."

The nurse had drawn away a little distance with the child. The rest of the family were making their preparations inside the house. There was no one near to watch the singular little drama.

"You should not say that," he added; "we all feel you to be one of us."

"But all your world does not feel me to be one of them," she rejoined.

"We shall see about that when you go up

to town. You are a bit morbid, Lali. I don't wonder at your feeling a little shy; but then you will simply carry things before you—now you take my word for it! For I know London pretty well."

She held out her ungloved hands.

"Do they compare with the white hands of the ladies you know?" she said. ·

"They are about the finest hands I have ever seen," he replied. "You can't see yourself, sister of mine."

"I do not care very much to see myself," she said. "If I had not a maid I expect I should look very shiftless, for I don't care to look in a mirror. My only mirror used to be a stream of water in summer," she added, "and a corner of a looking-glass got from the Hudson's Bay fort in the winter."

"Well, you are missing a lot of enjoyment," he said, "if you do not use your mirror much. The rest of us can appreciate what you would see there."

She reached out and touched his arm.

"Do you like to look at me?" she questioned, with a strange simple candour.

For the first time in many a year, Richard Armour blushed like a girl fresh from school. The question had come so suddenly, it had gone so quickly into a sensitive corner of his nature, that he lost command of himself for the instant, yet had little idea why the command was lost. He touched the fingers on his arm affectionately.

"Like to look at you?—like to look at you? Why, of course we all like to look at you. You are very fine and handsome—and interesting."

"Richard," she said, drawing her hands away, "is that why you like to look at me?"

He had recovered himself. He laughed in his old hearty way, and said—

"Yes, yes ; why, of course! Come, let us go and see the boy," he added, taking her arm and hurrying her down the steps. "Come and let us see Richard Joseph, the pride of all the Armours."

She moved beside him in a kind of dream. She had learned much since she came to Grey-hope, and yet she could not at that moment have told exactly why she asked Richard the question that had confused him, nor did she know quite what lay behind the question. But every problem which has life works itself out to its appointed end, if fumbling human fingers do not meddle with it. Half the miseries of this world are caused by forcing issues, in every problem of the affections, the emotions, and the soul. There is a law working with which there should be no tampering, lest in foolish interruption come only confusion and disaster. Against

105

every such question there should be written the one word, "Wait."

Richard Armour stooped over the child. "A beauty," he said, "a perfect little gentleman. Like Richard Joseph Armour there is none," he added.

"Whom do you think he looks like, Richard?" she asked. This was a question she had never asked before since the child was born. Whom the child looked like every one knew; but within the past year and a half Francis Armour's name had seldom been mentioned, and never in connection with the child. The child's mother asked the question with a strange quietness. Richard answered it without hesitation.

"The child looks like Frank," he said. "As like him as can be."

"I am glad," she said, "for all your sakes."

"You are very deep this morning, Lali," Richard said, with a kind of helplessness. "Frank will be pretty proud of the youngster when he comes back. But he won't be prouder of him than I am."

"I know that," she said. "Won't you be lonely without the boy—and me, Richard?"

Again the question went home. "Lonely? I should think I would," he said,—"I should think I would. But then, you see, school is over, and the master stays behind and makes

up the marks. You will find London a jollier
master than I am, Lali. There'll be lots of
shows, and plenty to do, and smart frocks, and
no end of feeds and frolics ; and that is more
amusing than studying three hours a day with
a dry old stick like me. I tell you what, when
Frank comes "—

She interrupted him. "Do not speak of that,"
she said. Then, with a sudden burst of feeling,
though her words were scarcely audible, "I owe
you everything, Richard—everything that is
good. I owe him nothing, Richard—nothing
but what is bitter."

"Hush, hush," he said ; "you must not speak
that way. Lali, I want to say to you "—

At that moment General Armour, Mrs. Armour,
and Marion appeared on the doorstep, and the
carriage came wheeling up the drive. What
Richard intended to say was left unsaid. The
chances were it never would be said.

"Well, well," said General Armour, calling
down at them, "escort his imperial highness to
the chariot which awaits him, and then ho!
for London town. Come along, my daughter,"
he said to Lali; "come up here and take the last
whiff of Greyhope that you will have for six
months. Dear, dear! what lunatics we all are,
to be sure! Why, we're as happy as little birds
in their nests out in the decent country, and yet

we scamper off to a smoky old city by the
Thames to rush along with the world, instead
of sitting high and far away from it and watching it go by. God bless my soul! I'm old enough
to know better. Well, let me help you in, my
dear," he added to his wife; "and in you go,
Marion; and in you go, your imperial highness,"
—he passed the child awkwardly in to Marion;
"and in you go, my daughter," he added, as
he handed Lali in, pressing her hand with a
brusque fatherliness as he did so. He then got
in after them.

Richard came to the side of the carriage and
bade them all good-bye one by one. Lali gave
him her hand, but did not speak a word. He
called a cheerful adieu, the horses were whipped
up, and in a moment Richard was left alone on
the steps of the house. He stood for a time
looking, then he turned to go into the house,
but changed his mind, sat down, lit a cigar, and
did not move from his seat until he was summoned to his lonely luncheon.

Nobody thought much of leaving Richard
behind at Greyhope. It seemed the natural
thing to do. But still he had not been left alone
—entirely alone—for three years or more.

The days and weeks went on. If Richard
had been accounted eccentric before, there was
far greater cause for the term now. Life dragged

Too much had been taken out of his life all at once; for, in the first place, the family had been drawn together more during the trouble which Lali's advent had brought; then the child and its mother, his pupil, were gone also. He wandered about in a kind of vague unrest. The hardest thing in this world to get used to is the absence of a familiar footstep and the cheerful greeting of a familiar eye. And the man with no chick or child feels even the absence of his dog from the hearthrug when he returns from a journey or his day's work. It gives him a sense of strangeness and loss. But when it is the voice of a woman and the hand of a child that is missed, you can back no speculation upon that man's mood or mind or conduct. There is no influence like the influence of habit, and that is how, when the minds of people are at one, physical distances and differences, no matter how great, are invisible, or at least not obvious.

Richard Armour was a sensible man; but when one morning he suddenly packed a portmanteau and went up to town to Cavendish Square, the act might be considered from two sides of the equation. If he came back to enter again into the social life which, for so many years, he had abjured, it was not very sensible, because the world never welcomes its deserters;

it might, if men and women grew younger instead of older. If he came to see his family, or because he hungered for his godchild, or because—but we are hurrying the situation. It were wiser not to state the problem yet. The afternoon that he arrived at Cavendish Square all his family were out except his brother's wife. Lali was in the drawing-room, receiving a visitor who had asked for Mrs. Armour and Mrs. Francis Armour. The visitor was received by Mrs. Francis Armour. The visitor knew that Mrs. Armour was not at home. She had by chance seen her and Marion in Bond Street, and was not seen by them. She straightway got into her carriage and drove up to Cavendish Square, hoping to find Mrs. Francis Armour at home. There had been house-parties at Greyhope since Lali had come there to live, but this visitor, though once an intimate friend of the family, had never been a guest.

The visitor was Lady Haldwell, once Miss Julia Sherwood, who had made possible what was called Francis Armour's tragedy. Since Lali had come to town Lady Haldwell had seen her, but had never met her. She was not at heart wicked, but there are few women who can resist an opportunity of anatomising and reckoning up the merits and demerits of a woman who has married an old lover. When that woman is in the position of Mrs. Francis Armour, the situation has an unusual piquancy and interest. Hence Lady Haldwell's journey of inquisition to Cavendish Square.

As Richard passed the drawing-room door to ascend the stairs, he recognised the voices.

Once a sort of heathen, as Mrs. Francis Armour had been, she still could grasp the situation with considerable clearness. There is nothing keener than one woman's instinct regarding another woman, where a man is concerned. Mrs. Francis Armour received Lady Haldwell with a quiet stateliness, which, if it did not astonish her, gave her sufficient warning that matters were not, in this little comedy, to be all her own way.

Thrown upon the mere resources of wit and language, Mrs. Francis Armour must have been at a disadvantage. For Lady Haldwell had a good gift of speech, a pretty talent for epithet, and no unnecessary tenderness. She bore Lali no malice. She was too decorous and high for that. In her mind the wife of the man she had discarded was a mere commonplace catastrophe, to be viewed without horror, maybe with pity. She had heard the alien spoken well of by some people ; others had seemed indignant that the Armours should try to push "a red woman" into English society. Truth is, the Armours did not try at all to push her. For over three years they had let society talk. They had not entertained largely in Cavendish Square since Lali came, and those invited to Greyhope had a chance to refuse the invitations if they chose. Most people did not choose to decline them. But Lady Haldwell was not of that number. She had never been invited. But now in town, when entertainment must be more general, she and the Armours were prepared for social interchange.

Behind Lady Haldwell's visits curiosity chiefly ran. She was in a way sorry for Frank Armour, for she had been fond of him after a fashion, always fonder of him than of Lord Haldwell. She had married with her fingers holding the scales of advantage ; and Lord Haldwell dressed well, was immensely rich, and the title had a charm.

When Mrs. Francis Armour met her with her strange, impressive dignity, she was the slightest bit confused, but not outwardly. She had not expected it. At first Lali did not know who her visitor was. She had not caught the name distinctly from the servant.

Presently Lady Haldwell said, as Lali gave her hand—

" I am Lady Haldwell. As Miss Sherwood I was an old friend of your husband."

A scornful glitter came into Mrs. Armour's eyes—a peculiar touch of burnished gold, an effect of the light at a certain angle of the lens. It gave for the instant an uncanny look to the face, almost something malicious. She guessed why this woman had come. She knew the whole history of the past, and it touched her in a tender spot. She knew she was had at an advantage. Before her was a woman perfectly trained in the fine social life to which she was born, whose equanimity was as regular as her features. Herself was by nature a creature of impulse, of the woods and streams and open life. The social convention had been engrafted. As yet she was used to thinking and speaking with all candour. She was to have her training in the charms of superficiality, but that was to come ; and when it came she would not be an unskilful apprentice. Perhaps the latent subtlety of her race came to help her natural candour at the moment. For she said at once, in a slow, quiet tone—

"I never heard my husband speak of you. Will you sit down ? "

"And Mrs. Armour and Marion are not in ? No, I suppose your husband did not speak much of his old friends."

The attack was studied and cruel. But Lady Haldwell had been stung by Mrs. Armour's

H                                113

remark, and it piqued her that this was possible.

"Oh yes, he spoke of some of his friends, but not of you."

"Indeed! That is strange."

"There was no necessity," said Mrs. Armour quietly.

"Of discussing me? I suppose not. But by some chance"—

"It was just as well, perhaps, not to anticipate the pleasure of our meeting."

Lady Haldwell was surprised  She had not expected this cleverness. They talked casually for a little time, the visitor trying in vain to delicately give the conversation a personal turn. At last, a little foolishly, she grew bolder, with a needless selfishness.

"So old a friend of your husband as I am, I am hopeful you and I may be friends also."

Mrs. Armour saw the move.

"You are very kind," she said conventionally, and offered a cup of tea.

Lady Haldwell now ventured unwisely. She was nettled at the other's self-possession.

"But then, in a way, I have been your friend for a long time, Mrs. Armour."

The point was veiled in a vague tone, but Mrs. Armour understood. Her reply was not wanting.

"Any one who has been a friend to my husband has, naturally, claims upon me."

Lady Haldwell, in spite of herself, chafed. There was a subtlety in the woman before her not to be reckoned with lightly.

"And if an enemy?" she said, smiling.

A strange smile also flickered across Mrs. Armour's face as she said—

"If an enemy of my husband called, and was penitent, I should — offer her tea, no doubt."

"That is, in this country; but in your own country, which, I believe, is different, what would you do?"

Mrs. Armour looked steadily and coldly into her visitor's eyes.

"In my country enemies do not compel us to be polite."

"By calling on you?" Lady Haldwell was growing a little reckless. "But then, that is a savage country. We are different here. I suppose, however, your husband told you of these things, so that you were not surprised. And when does he come? His stay is protracted. Let me see, how long is it? Ah yes, near four years." Here she became altogether reckless, which she regretted afterwards, for she knew, after all, what was due herself. "He *will* come back, I suppose?"

Lady Haldwell was no coward, else she had hesitated before speaking in that way before this woman, in whose blood was the wildness of the heroical North. Perhaps she guessed the passion in Lali's breast, perhaps not. In any case she would have said what she listed at the moment.

Wild as were the passions in Lali's breast, she thought on the instant of her child, of what Richard Armour would say; for he had often talked to her about not showing her emotions and passions, had told her that violence of all kinds was not wise or proper. Her fingers ached to grasp this beautiful, exasperating woman by the throat. But after an effort at calmness she remained still and silent, looking at her visitor with a scornful dignity. Lady Haldwell presently rose,—she could not endure the furnace of that look,—and said good-bye. She turned towards the door. Mrs. Armour remained immovable. At that instant, however, some one stepped from behind a large screen just inside the door. It was Richard Armour. He was pale, and on his face was a sternness the like of which this and perhaps only one other woman had ever seen on him. He interrupted her.

"Lady Haldwell has a fine talent for irony," he said, " but she does not always use it wisely.

In a man it would bear another name, and from a man it would be differently received." He came close to her. "You are a brave woman," he said, "or you would have been more careful. Of course you knew that my mother and sister were not at home?"

She smiled languidly. "And why 'of course'?"

"I do not know that; only I know that I think so; and I also think that my brother Frank's worst misfortune did not occur when Miss Julia Sherwood trafficked without compunction in his happiness."

"Don't be oracular, my dear Richard Armour," she said; "you are trying, really. This seems almost melodramatic; and melodrama is bad enough at Drury Lane."

"You are not a good friend even to yourself," he answered.

"What a discoverer you are! And how much in earnest! Do come back to the world, Mr. Armour; you would be a relief, a new sensation."

"I fancy I shall come back, if only to see the 'engineer hoist with his own'—torpedo."

He paused before the last word to give it point, for her husband's father had made his money out of torpedoes. She felt the sting in spite of herself, and she saw the point.

"And then we will talk it over at the end of the season," he added, "and compare notes. Good-afternoon."

"You stake much on your hazard," she said, glancing back at Lali, who still stood immovable. *Au revoir!*"

She left the room. Richard heard the door close after her and the servant retire. Then he turned to Lali.

As he did so, she ran forward to him with a cry. "Oh, Richard, Richard!" she said, with a sob, threw her arms over his shoulder, and let her forehead drop on his breast. Then came a sudden impulse in his blood. Long after he shuddered when he remembered what he thought at that instant; what he wished to do; what rich madness possessed him. He knew now why he had come to town; he also knew why he must not stay, or, if staying, what must be his course.

He took her gently by the arm and led her to a chair, speaking cheerily to her. Then he sat down beside her, and all at once again, her face wet and burning, she flung herself forward on her knees beside him, and clung to him.

"Oh, Richard, I am glad you have come," she said. "I would have killed her if I had not thought of you. I want you to stay; I am always better when you are with me. I have

118

missed you, and I know that baby misses you too."

He had his cue. He rose, trembling a little. "Come, come," he said heartily, "it's all right, it's all right—my sister. Let us go and see the youngster. There, dry your eyes, and forget all about that woman. She is only envious of you. Come, for his imperial highness!"

She was in a tumult of feeling. It was seldom that she had shown emotion in the past two years, and it was the more ample when it did break forth. But she dried her eyes, and together they went to the nursery. She dismissed the nurse, and they were left alone by the sleeping child. She knelt at the head of the little cot, and touched the child's forehead with her lips. He stooped down also beside it.

"He's a grand little fellow," he said. "Lali," he continued presently, "it is time Frank came home. I am going to write for him. If he does not come at once, I shall go and fetch him."

"Never! never!" Her eyes flashed angrily. "Promise that you will not. Let him come when he is ready. He does not care." She shuddered a little.

"But he will care when he comes, and you— you care for him, Lali?"

Again she shuddered, and a whiteness ran under the hot excitement of her cheeks. She

119

said nothing, but looked up at him, then dropped her face in her hands.

"You do care for him, Lali," he said earnestly, almost solemnly, his lips twitching slightly. "You must care for him; it is his right; and he will—I swear to you I know he will—care for you."

In his own mind there was another thought, a hard, strange thought; and it had to do with the possibility of his brother not caring for this wife.

Still she did not speak.

"To a good woman, with a good husband," he continued, "there is no one—there should be no one—like the father of her child. And no woman ever loved her child more than you do yours." He knew that this was special pleading.

She trembled, and then dropped her cheek beside the child's. "I want Frank to be happy," he went on; "there is no one I care more for than for Frank."

She lifted her face to him now, in it a strange light. Then her look ran to confusion, and she seemed to read all that he meant to convey. He knew she did. He touched her shoulder.

"You must do the best you can every way, for Frank's sake, for all our sakes. I will help you—God knows I will—all I can."

"Oh yes, yes," she said, from the child's pillow. He could see the flame in her cheek. "I understand." She put out her hand to him, but did not look up. "Leave me alone with my baby, Richard," she pleaded.

He took her hand and pressed it again and again in his old, unconscious way. Then he let it go, and went slowly to the door. There he turned and looked back at her. He mastered the hot thought in him.

"God help me!" she murmured from the cot.

The next morning Richard went back to Greyhope.

# CHAPTER VII

## A COURT-MARTIAL

IT was hard to tell, save for a certain deliberateness of speech and a colour a little more pronounced than that of a Spanish woman, that Mrs. Frank Armour had not been brought up in England. She had a kind of grave sweetness and distant charm which made her notable at any table or in any ballroom. Indeed, it soon became apparent that she was to be the pleasant talk, the interest of the season. This was tolerably comforting to the Armours. Again Richard's prophecy had been fulfilled, and as he sat alone at Greyhope and read the *Morning Post*, noticing Lali's name at distinguished gatherings, or, picking up the *World*, saw how the lion-hunters talked extravagantly of her, he took some satisfaction to himself that he had foreseen her triumph where others looked for her downfall. Lali herself was not elated ; it gratified her, but she had been an angel, and a very unsatisfactory one, if it had not done so. As her confidence grew (though outwardly she had never appeared to lack it greatly), she did not hesitate to speak of herself as an Indian, her country as a good country, and her people as a noble if dispossessed race ; all the more so if she thought reference to her nationality and past was being rather conspicuously avoided. She had asked General Armour for an interview with her husband's solicitor. This was granted. When she met the solicitor, she asked him to send no newspaper to her husband containing any reference to herself, nor yet to mention her in his letters.

She had never directly received a line from him but once, and that was after she had come to know the truth about his marriage with her. She could read in the conventional sentences, made simple as for a child, the strained politeness, and his absolute silence as to whether or not a child had been born to them, the utter absence of affection for her. She had also induced General Armour and his wife to give her husband's solicitor no information regarding the birth of the child. There was thus apparently no more inducement for him to hurry back to England than there was when he had sent her off on his mission of retaliation, which had been such an ignominious failure.

For the humiliation of his family had been short-lived, the affront to Lady Haldwell nothing at all. The Armours had not been human if they had failed to enjoy their daughter-in-law's success. Although they never, perhaps, would quite recover the disappointment concerning Lady Agnes Martling, the result was so much better than they in their cheerfullest moments dared hope for, that they appeared genuinely content.

To their grandchild they were devotedly attached. Marion was his faithful slave and admirer, so much so that Captain Vidall, who now and then was permitted to see the child, declared himself jealous; he and Marion were to be married soon. The wedding had been delayed owing to his enforced absence abroad. Mrs. Edward Lambert, once Mrs. Townley, shyly regretted in Lali's presence that the child, or one as sweet, was not hers. Her husband evidently shared her opinion, from the extraordinary notice he took of it when his wife was not present. Not that Richard Joseph Armour, Jun., was always *en évidence*, but when asked for by his faithful friends and admirers he was amiably produced.

Meanwhile, Frank Armour across the sea was engaged with many things. His business concerns had not prospered prodigiously, chiefly

because his judgment, like his temper, had grown
somewhat uncertain. His popularity in the
Hudson's Bay country had been at some tension
since he had shipped his wife away to England.
Even the ordinary savage mind saw something
unusual and undomestic in it, and the general
hospitality declined a little. Armour did not
immediately guess the cause ; but one day, about
a year after his wife had gone, he found occasion
to reprove a half-breed, by name Jacques
Pontiac ; and Jacques, with more honesty than
politeness, said some hard words, and asked
how much he paid for his English hired devils
to kill his wife. Strange to say, he did not
resent this startling remark. It set him thinking.
He began to blame himself for not having
written oftener to his people—and to his wife.
He wondered how far his revenge had succeeded.
He was most ashamed of it now. He knew that
he had done a dishonourable thing. The more
he thought upon it the more angry with himself
he became. Yet he dreaded to go back to
England and face it all: the reproach of his
people ; the amusement of society ; his wife
herself. He never attempted to picture her
as a civilised being. He scarcely knew her
when he married her. She knew him much
better, for primitive people are quicker in the
play of their passions, and she had come to
125

love him before he had begun to notice her at all.

Presently he ate his heart out with mortification. To be yoked for ever to—a savage! It was horrible! And their children? It was strange he had not thought of that before. Children? He shrugged his shoulders. There might possibly be a child, but children—never! But he doubted even regarding a child, for no word had come to him concerning that possibility. He was even most puzzled at the tone and substance of their letters. From the beginning there had been no reproaches, no excitement, no railing, but studied kindness and conventional statements, through which Mrs. Armour's solicitous affection scarcely ever peeped. He had shot his bolt, and got—consideration, almost imperturbability. They appeared to treat the matter as though he were a wild youth who would not yet mend his ways. He read over their infrequent letters to him; his to them had been still more infrequent. In one there was the statement that "she was progressing favourably with her English"; in another, that "she was riding a good deal"; again, that "she appeared anxious to adapt herself to her new life."

At all these he whistled a little to himself, and smiled bitterly. Then, all at once, he got up and straightway burned them all. He again tried to put the matter behind him for the present, knowing that he must face it one day, and staving off its reality as long as possible. He did his utmost to be philosophical and say his *quid refert*, but it was easier tried than done; for Jacques Pontiac's words kept rankling in his mind, and he found himself carrying round a vague load, which made him abstracted occasionally, and often a little reckless in action and speech. In hunting bear and moose he had proved himself more daring than the oldest hunter, and proportionately successful. He paid his servants well, but was sharp with them.

He made long, hard expeditions, defying the weather as the hardiest of prairie and mountain men mostly hesitate to defy it; he bought up much land, then, dissatisfied, sold it again at a loss, but subsequently made final arrangements for establishing a very large farm. When he once became actually interested in this he shook off something of his moodiness and settled himself to develop the thing. He had good talent for initiative and administration, and at last, in the time when his wife was a feature of the London season, he found his scheme in working order, and the necessity of going to England was forced upon him.

Actually he wished that the absolute necessity

had presented itself before. There was always the moral necessity, of course—but then! Here now was a business need; and he must go. Yet he did not fix a day or make definite arrangements. He could hardly have believed himself such a coward. With liberal emphasis he called himself a sneak, and one day at Fort Charles sat down to write to his solicitor in Montreal to say that he would come on at once. Still he hesitated. As he sat there thinking, Eye-of-the-Moon, his father-in-law, opened the door quietly and entered. He had avoided the chief ever since he had come back to Fort Charles, and practically had not spoken to him for a year. Armour flushed slightly with annoyance. But presently, with a touch of his old humour, he rose, held out his hand, and said ironically, "Well, father-in-law, it's about time we had a big talk, isn't it? We are not very intimate for such close relatives."

The old Indian did not fully understand the meaning or the tone of Armour's speech, but he said, "*How!*" and, reaching out his hand for the pipe offered him, lighted it, and sat down, smoking in silence. Armour waited; but, seeing that the other was not yet moved to talk, he turned to his letter again. After a time, Eye-of-the-Moon said gravely, getting to his feet, "Brother!"

Armour looked up, then rose also. The Indian bowed to him courteously, then sat down again. Armour threw a leg over a corner of the table and waited.

"Brother," said the Indian presently, "you are of the great race that conquers us. You come and take our land and our game, and we at last have to beg of you for food and shelter. Then you take our daughters, and we know not where they go. They are gone like the down from the thistle. We see them not, but you remain. And men say evil things. There are bad words abroad. Brother, what have you done with my daughter?"

Had the Indian come and stormed, begged money of him, sponged on him, or abused him, he had taken it very calmly,—he, in fact, had been superior. But there was dignity in the chief's manner; there was solemnity in his speech; his voice conveyed resoluteness and earnestness, which the stoic calm of his face might not have suggested; and Armour felt that he had no advantage at all. Besides, Armour had a conscience, though he had played some rare tricks with it of late, and it needed more hardihood than he possessed to face this old man down. And why face him down? Lali was his daughter, blood of his blood, the chieftainess of one branch of his people,

I                129

honoured at least among these poor savages, and the old man had a right to ask, as asked another more famous, " Where is my daughter ? "

His hands in his pockets, Armour sat silent for a minute, eyeing his boot, as he swung his leg to and fro. Presently he said, " Eye-of-the-Moon, I don't think I can talk as poetically as you, even in my own language, and I shall not try. But I should like to ask you this : Do you believe any harm has come to your daughter— to my wife ? "

The old Indian forgot to blow the tobacco-smoke from his mouth, and, as he sat debating, lips slightly apart, it came leaking out in little trailing clouds and gave a strange appearance to his iron-featured face. He looked steadily at Armour, and said, " You are of those who rule in your land,"—here Armour protested,— "you have much gold to buy and sell. I am a chief,"—he drew himself up,—" I am poor: we speak with the straight tongue; it is cowards who lie. Speak deep as from the heart, my brother, and tell me where my daughter is."

Armour could not but respect the chief for the way this request was put, but still it galled him to think that he was under suspicion of having done any bodily injury to his wife, so he quietly persisted : " Do you think I have done Lali any harm ? "

"The thing is strange," replied the other. "You are of those who are great among your people. You married a daughter of a red man. Then she was yours for less than one moon, and you sent her far away, and you stayed. Her father was as a dog in your sight. Do men whose hearts are clear act so? They have said strange things of you. I have not believed; but it is good I know all, that I may say to the tale-bearers, 'You have crooked tongues.'"

Armour sat for a moment longer, his face turned to the open window. He was perfectly still, but he had become grave. He was about to reply to the chief, when the trader entered the room hurriedly with a newspaper in his hand. He paused abruptly when he saw Eye-of-the-Moon. Armour felt that the trader had something important to communicate. He guessed it was in the paper. He mutely held out his hand for it. The trader handed it to him hesitatingly, at the same time pointing to a paragraph, and saying, "It is nearly two years old, as you see. I chanced upon it by accident to-day."

It was a copy of a London evening paper, containing a somewhat sensational account of Lali's accident. It said that she was in a critical condition. This time Armour did not ask for brandy, but the trader put it out beside him. He shook his head. "Gordon," he said presently, "I shall leave here in the morning. Please send my men to me."

The trader whispered to him, "She was all right, of course, long ago, Mr. Armour, or you would have heard."

Armour looked at the date of the paper. He had several letters from England of a later date, and these said nothing of her illness. It bewildered him, made him uneasy. Perhaps the first real sense of his duty as a husband came home to him there. For the first time he was anxious about the woman for her own sake. The trader had left the room.

"What a scoundrel I've been!" said Armour between his teeth, oblivious, for the moment, of Eye-of-the-Moon's presence. Presently, bethinking himself, he turned to the Indian. "I've been debating," he said. "Eye-of-the-Moon, my wife is in England, at my father's home. I am going to her. Men have lied in thinking I would do her any injury, but—but— never mind, the harm was of another kind. It isn't wise for a white man and an Indian to marry, but when they are married—well, they must live as man and wife should live, and, as I said, I am going to my wife—your daughter."

To say all this to a common Indian, whose only property was a half-dozen ponies and a couple of tepees, required something very like moral courage ; but then Armour had not been exercising moral courage during the last year or so, and its exercise was profitable to him. The next morning he was on his way to Montreal, and Eye-of-the-Moon was the richest chief in British North America, at that moment, by five thousand dollars or so.

# CHAPTER VIII

## TO EVERY MAN HIS HOUR

IT was the close of the season : many people
had left town, but festivities were still on. To
a stranger the season might have seemed at its
height. The Armours were giving a large party
in Cavendish Square before going back again
to Greyhope, where, for the sake of Lali and
her child, they intended to remain during the
rest of the summer, in preference to going on
the Continent or to Scotland. The only unsatisfactory feature of Lali's season was the
absence of her husband. Naturally there were
those who said strange things regarding Frank
Armour's stay in America; but it was pretty
generally known that he was engaged in land
speculations, and his club friends, who perhaps
took the pleasantest view of the matter, said
that he was very wise indeed, if a little cowardly
in staying abroad until his wife was educated
and ready to take her position in society.

There was one thing on which they were all agreed : Mrs. Frank Armour either had a mind superior to the charms of their sex, or was incapable of that vanity which hath many suitors, and says, "So far shalt thou go, and "— The fact is, Mrs. Frank Armour's mind was superior. She had only one object— to triumph over her husband grandly, as a woman righteously might. She had vanity, of course, but it was not ignoble. She kept one thing in view ; she lived for it. Her translation had been successful. There were times when she remembered her father, the wild days on the prairies, the buffalo-hunt, tracking the deer, tribal battles, the long silent hours of the winter, and the warm summer nights when she slept in the prairie grass or camped with her people in the trough of a great land-wave. Sometimes the hunger for its freedom, and its idleness, and its sport, came to her greatly ; but she thought of her child, and she put it from her. She was ambitious for him ; she was keen to prove her worth as a wife against her husband's unworthiness. This perhaps saved her. She might have lost had her life been without this motive.

The very morning of this notable reception, General Armour had received a note from Frank Armour's solicitor, saying that his son was likely to arrive in London from America

135

that day or the next. Frank had written to his people no word of his coming; to his wife, as we have said, he had not written for months; and before he started back he would not write, because he wished to make what amends he could in person. He expected to find her improved, of course, but still he could only think of her as an Indian, showing her common prairie origin. His knowledge of her before their marriage had been particularly brief; she was little more in his eyes than a thousand other Indian women, save that she was better-looking, was whiter than most, and had finer features. He could not very clearly remember the tones of her voice, because after marriage, and before he had sent her to England, he had seen little or nothing of her.

When General Armour received the news of Frank's return he told his wife and Marion, and they consulted together whether it were good to let Lali know at once. He might arrive that evening. If so, the position would be awkward, because it was impossible to tell how it might affect her. If they did tell her, and Frank happened not to arrive, it might unnerve her so as to make her appearance in the evening doubtful. Richard, the wiseacre, the inexhaustible Richard, was caring for his cottagers and cutting the leaves of new books

—his chiefest pleasure—at Greyhope. They felt it was a matter they ought to be able to decide for themselves, but still it was the last evening of Lali's stay in town, and they did not care to take any risk. Strange to say, they had come to take pride in their son's wife ; for even General and Mrs. Armour, high-minded and of serene social status as they were, seemed not quite insensible to the pleasure of being an axle on which a system of social notoriety revolved.

At the opportune moment Captain Vidall was announced, and, because he and Marion were soon to carry but one name between them, he was called into family consultation. It is somewhat singular that in this case the women were quite wrong and the men were quite right. For General Armour and Captain Vidall were for silence until Frank came, if he came that day, or for telling her the following morning, when the function was over. And the men prevailed.

Marion was much excited all day ; she had given orders that Frank's room should be made ready, but for whom she gave no information. While Lali was dressing for the evening, something excited and nervous, she entered her room. They were now the best of friends. The years had seen many shifting scenes in their com-

137

panionship; they had been as often at war as
at peace; but they had respected each other,
each after her own fashion; and now they had
a real and mutual regard. Lali's was a slim,
lithe figure, wearing its fashionable robes with
an air of possession; and the face above it, if
not entirely beautiful, had a strange, warm
fascination. The girl had not been a chieftainess for nothing. A look of quiet command
was there, but also a far-away expression which
gave a faint look of sadness even when a smile
was at the lips. The smile itself did not come
quickly, it grew; but above it all was hair of
perfect brown,—most rare,—setting off her face
as a plume does a helmet. She showed no
surprise when Marion entered. She welcomed
her with a smile and outstretched hand, but
said nothing.

"Lali," said Marion somewhat abruptly,—
she scarcely knew why she said it,—"are you
happy?"

It was strange how the Indian girl had taken
on those little manners of society which convey
so much by inflection. She lifted her eyebrows
at Marion, and said presently, in a soft, deliberate
voice, "Come, Marion, we will go and see little
Richard; then I shall be happy."

She linked her arm through Marion's. Marion
drummed her fingers lightly on the beautiful

138

arm, and then fell to wondering what she should say next. They passed into the room where the child lay sleeping; they went to his little bed, and Lali stretched out her hand gently, touching the curls of the child. Running a finger through one delicately, she said, with a still softer tone than before, " Why should not one be happy ? "

Marion looked up slowly into her eyes, let a hand fall on her shoulder gently, and replied, " Lali, do you never wish Frank to come ? "

Lali's fingers came from the child, the colour mounted slowly to her forehead, and she drew the girl away again into the other room. Then she turned and faced Marion, a deep fire in her eyes, and said, in a whisper almost hoarse in its intensity, " Yes ; I wish he would come to-night."

She looked harder yet at Marion; then, with a flash of pride and her hands clasping before her, she drew herself up, and added, " Am I not worthy to be his wife now ? Am I not beautiful —for a savage ? "

There was no common vanity in the action. It had a noble kind of wistfulness, and a serenity that entirely redeemed it. Marion dated her own happiness from the time when Lali met her accident, for in the evening of that disastrous day she issued to Captain Hume Vidall a com- mission which he could never—wished never—to

resign. Since then she had been at her best,—
we are all more or less selfish creatures,—and
had grown gentler, curbing the delicate imperi-
ousness of her nature, and frankly, and without
the least pique, taken a secondary position of
interest in the household, occasioned by Lali's
popularity. She looked Lali up and down with
a glance in which many feelings met, and then,
catching her hands warmly, she lifted them, put
them on her own shoulders, and said, " My dear
beautiful savage, you are fit and worthy to
be Queen of England ; and Frank, when he
comes "—

" Hush ! " said the other dreamily, and put a
finger on Marion's lips. " I know what you are
going to say, but I do not wish to hear it. He
did not love me then. He used me "— She
shuddered, put her hands to her eyes with a
pained, trembling motion, then threw her head
back with a quick sigh. " But I will not speak
of it. Come, we are for the dance, Marion. It is
the last, to-night. To-morrow "— She paused,
looking straight before her, lost in thought.

" Yes, to-morrow, Lali ? "

" I do not know about to-morrow," was the
reply. " Strange things come to me."

Marion longed to tell her then and there the
great news, but she was afraid to do so, and
was, moreover, withheld by the remembrance

that it had been agreed she should not be told. She said nothing.

At eleven o'clock the rooms were filled. For the fag end of the season, people seemed unusually brilliant. The evening itself was not so hot as common, and there was an extra array of distinguished guests. Marion was nervous all the evening, though she showed little of it, being most prettily employed in making people pleased with themselves. Mrs. Armour also was not free from apprehension. In reply to inquiries concerning her son she said, as she had often said during the season, that he might be back at any time now. Lali had answered always in the same fashion, and had shown no sign that his continued absence was singular. As the evening wore on, the probability of Frank's appearance seemed less; and the Armours began to breathe more freely.

Frank had, however, arrived. He had driven straight from Euston to Cavendish Square, but, seeing the house lighted up, and guests arriving, he had a sudden feeling of uncertainty. He ordered the cabman to take him to his club. There he put himself in evening-dress, and drove back again to the house. He entered quietly. At the moment the hall was almost deserted; people were mostly in the ballroom and supper-room. He paused a moment, biting

141

his moustache as if in perplexity. A strange
timidity came on him. All his old dash and
self-possession seemed to have forsaken him.
Presently, seeing a number of people entering
the hall, he made for the staircase, and went
hastily up. Mechanically he went to his own
room, and found it lighted. Flowers were set
about, and everything was made ready as for
a guest. He sat down, not thinking, but dazed.
Glancing up, he saw his face in a mirror. It
was bronzed, but it looked rather old and care-
worn. He shrugged a shoulder at that. Then,
in the mirror, he saw also something else. It
startled him so that he sat perfectly still for a
moment looking at it. It was some one laughing
at him over his shoulder—a child! He got to
his feet and turned round. On the table was a
very large photograph of a smiling child—with
*his* eyes, *his* face. He caught the chair-arm,
and stood looking at it a little wildly. Then
he laughed a strange laugh, and the tears leaped
to his eyes. He caught the picture in his hands,
and kissed it,—very foolishly, men not fathers
might think, — and read the name beneath,
Richard Joseph Armour ; and again, beneath
that, the date of birth. He then put it back on
the table and sat looking at it—looking, and
forgetting, and remembering.

Presently the door opened, and some one

entered. It was Marion. She had seen him pass through the hall ; she had then gone and told her father and mother, to prepare them, and had followed him upstairs. He did not hear her. She stepped softly forward. "Frank!" she said,—"Frank!" and laid a hand on his shoulder. He started up and turned his face on her. Then he caught her hands and kissed her. "Marion!" he said, and he could say no more. But presently he pointed towards the photograph.

She nodded her head. "Yes, it is your child, Frank. Though, of course, you don't deserve it. . . . Frank dear," she added, "I am glad—we shall all be glad—to have you back ; but you are a wicked man." She felt she must say that.

Now he only nodded, and still looked at the portrait. "Where is—my wife?" he added presently.

"She is in the ballroom." Marion was wondering what was best to do.

He caught his thumb-nail in his teeth. He winced in spite of himself. "I will go to her," he said, "and then—the baby."

"I am glad," she replied, "that you have so much sense of justice left, Frank: the wife first, the baby afterwards. But do you think you deserve either?"

He became moody, and made an impatient

gesture. "Lady Agnes Martling is here, and also Lady Haldwell," she persisted cruelly. She did not mind, because she knew he would have enough to compensate him afterwards.

"Marion," he said, "say it all, and let me have it over. Say what you like, and I'll not whimper. I'll face it. But I want to see my child."

She was sorry for him. She had really wanted to see how much he was capable of feeling in the matter. "Wait here, Frank," she said. "That will be best ; and I will bring your wife to you."

He said nothing, but assented with a motion of the hand, and she left him where he was. He braced himself for the interview. Assuredly a man loses something of natural courage and self-confidence when he has done a thing of which he should be, and is, ashamed.

It seemed a long time (it was in reality but a couple of minutes) before the door opened again, and Marion said, "Frank, your wife!" and then retreated.

The door closed, leaving a stately figure standing just inside it. The figure did not move forward, but stood there, full of life and fine excitement, but very still also.

Frank Armour was confounded. He came forward slowly, looking hard. Was this distinguished, handsome, reproachful woman his wife, — Lali, the Indian girl, whom he had married in a fit of pique and brandy? He could hardly believe his eyes; and yet hers looked out at him with something that he remembered too, together with something which he did not remember, making him uneasy. Clearly, his great mistake had turned from ashes into fruit. " Lali, my wife !" he said, and held out his hand.

She reached out hers courteously, but her fingers gave him no response.

" We have many things to say to each other," she said, " but they cannot be said now. I shall be missed from the ballroom."

" Missed from the ballroom?" He almost laughed to think how strange this sounded in his ears. As if interpreting his thought, she added, "You see, it is our last affair of the season, and we are all anxious to do our duty perfectly. Will you go down with me? We can talk afterwards."

Her continued self-possession utterly confused him. She had utterly confused Marion also, when told that her husband was in the house. She had had presentiments, and, besides, she had been schooling herself for this hour for a long time. She turned towards the door.

" But," he asked, like a supplicant, " our child ! I want to see our child."

K                    145

She lifted her eyebrows, then, seeing the
photograph of the baby on the table, understood how he knew. "Come with me, then,"
she said, with a little more feeling.

She led the way along the landing, and paused
at her door. "Remember that we have to
appear amongst the guests directly," she said,
as though to warn him against. any demon-
stration. Then they entered. She went over
to the cot and drew back the fleecy curtain
from over the sleeping boy's head. His fingers
hungered to take his child to his arms. "He is
magnificent! magnificent!" he said, with a great
pride. "Why did you never let me know of it?"

"How could I tell what you would do?" she
calmly replied. "You married me—wickedly,
and used me wickedly afterwards; and I loved
the child."

"You loved the child?" he repeated after her.
"Lali," he said, "I don't deserve it, but forgive
me, if you can—for the child's sake."

"We had better go below," she calmly replied;
"we have both duties to do. You will of course
—appear with me—before them?"

The slight irony in the tone cut him horribly.
He offered his arm in silence. They passed
on to the staircase.

"It is necessary," she said, "to appear cheerful
before one's guests."

She had him at an advantage at every point. "We will be cheerful, then," was his reply, spoken with a grim kind of humour. "You have learned it all, haven't you?" he added.

They were just entering the ballroom. "Yes, with your kind help—and absence," she replied.

The surprise of the guests was somewhat diminished by the fact that Marion, telling General Armour and his wife first of Frank's return, industriously sent the news buzzing about the room.

The two went straight to Frank's father and mother. Their parts were all excellently played. Then Frank mingled among the guests, being very heartily greeted, and heard congratulations on all sides. Old club friends rallied him as a deserter, and new acquaintances flocked about him; and presently he awakened to the fact that his Indian wife had been an interest of the season, was not the least admired person present. It was altogether too good luck for him; but he had an uncomfortable conviction that he had a long path of penance to walk before he could hope to enjoy it.

All at once he met Lady Haldwell, who, in spite of all, still accepted invitations to General Armour's house—the strange scene between Lali and herself never having been disclosed to the family. He had nothing but bitterness in his heart for her, but he spoke a few smooth words, and she languidly congratulated him on his bronzed appearance. He asked for a dance, but she had not one to give him. As she was leaving, she suddenly turned as though she had forgotten something, and looking at him, said, " I forgot to congratulate you on your marriage. I hope it is not too late?"                    ·

He bowed. "Your congratulations are so sincere," he said, "that they would be *à propos* late or early."

When he stood with his wife whilst the guests were leaving, and saw with what manner she carried it all off,—as though she had been born in the good land of good breeding,—he was moved alternately with wonder and shame— shame that he had intended this noble creature as a sacrifice to his ugly temper and spite.

When all the guests were gone and the family stood alone in the drawing-room, a silence suddenly fell amongst them. Presently Marion said to her mother in a half-whisper, "I wish Richard were here."

They all felt the extreme awkwardness of the situation, especially when Lali bade General Armour, Mrs. Armour, and Marion good-night, and then, turning to her husband, said, "Good- night,"--she did not even speak his name. "Perhps you would care to ride to-morrow morning? I always go to the Park at ten, and this will be my last ride of the season."

Had she written out an elaborate proclamation of her intended attitude towards her husband, it could not have more clearly conveyed her mind than this little speech, delivered as to a most friendly acquaintance. General Armour pulled his moustache fiercely, and, it is possible, enjoyed the situation, despite its peril. Mrs. Armour turned to the mantel and seemed tremulously engaged in arranging some bric-à-brac. Marion, however, with a fine instinct, slid her arm through that of Lali, and gently said, " Yes, of course Frank will be glad of a ride in the Park. He used to ride with me every morning. But let us go, us three, and kiss the baby good-night, —' good-night till we meet in the morning.'"

She linked her arm now through Frank's, and as she did so he replied to Lali, " I shall be glad to ride in the morning, but "—

" But we can arrange it at breakfast," said his wife hurriedly. At the same time she allowed herself to be drawn away to the hall with her husband.

He was very angry, but he knew he had no right to be so. He choked back his wrath and moved on amiably enough, and suddenly the fashion in which the tables had been turned on him struck him with its tragic comedy, and he involuntarily smiled. His sense of humour saved him from words and acts which might possibly have made the matter a pure tragedy after all. He loosed his arm from Marion's.

"I must bid our father and mother good-night. Then I will join you both—'in the court of the king.'" And he turned and went back, and said to his father as he kissed his mother, "I am had at an advantage, General."

"And serves you right, my boy. You had the odds with you ; she has captured them like a born soldier."

His mother said to him gently, "Frank, you blamed us, but remember that we wished only your good. Take my advice, dear, and try to love your wife and win her confidence."

"Love her—*try* to love her?" he said. "I shall easily do that. But the other——?" He shook his head a little, though what he meant perhaps he did not know quite himself, and then followed Marion and Lali upstairs. Marion had tried to escape from Lali, but was told that she must stay ; and the three met at the child's cot. Marion stooped down and kissed its forehead. Frank stooped also and kissed its cheek. Then the wife kissed the other cheek. The child slept peacefully on.

"You can always see the baby here before breakfast, if you choose," said Lali ; and she held out her hand again in good-night. At this point Marion stole away, in spite of Lali's quick little cry of "Wait, Marion!" and the two were left alone again.

"I am very tired," she said. "I would rather not talk to-night." The dismissal was evident.

He took her hand, held it an instant, and presently said, "I will not detain you, but I would ask you, Lali, to remember that you are my wife. Nothing can alter that."

"Still we are only strangers, as you know," she quietly rejoined.

"You forget the days we were together—after we were married," he cautiously urged.

"I am not the same girl, . . . you killed her. . . . We have to start again. . . . I know all."

"You know that in my wretched anger and madness I"—

"Oh, please do not speak of it," she said; "it is so bad even in thought."

"But will you never forgive me, and care for me?—we have to live our lives together."

"Pray let us not speak of it now," she said, in a weary voice; then, breathlessly, "It is of much more consequence that you should love me—and the child."

He drew himself up with a choking sigh, and spread out his arms to her. "Oh, my wife!" he said.

"No, no," she cried, "this is unreasonable; we know so little of each other. . . . Good-night, again."

He turned at the door, came back, and, stooping, kissed the child on the lips. Then he said, "You are right. I deserve to suffer. . . . Good-night."

But when he was gone she dropped on her knees, and kissed the child many times on the lips also.

# CHAPTER IX

## THE FAITH OF COMRADES

WHEN Francis Armour left his wife's room
he did not go to his own, but quietly descended the stairs, went to the library, and sat
down. The loneliest thing in the world is to be
*tête-à-tête* with one's conscience. A man may
have a bad hour with an enemy, a sad hour with
a friend, a peaceful hour with himself, but when
the little dwarf, conscience, perches upon every
hillock of remembrance and makes slow signs
—those strange symbols of the language of the
soul—to him, no slave upon the treadmill suffers
more.

The butler came in to see if anything was
required, but Armour only greeted him silently
and waved him away. His brain was painfully
alert, his memory singularly awake. It seemed
that the incident of this hour had so opened up
every channel of his intelligence that all his life
ran past him in fantastic panorama, as by that

illumination which comes to the drowning man. He seemed under some strange spell. Once or twice he rose, rubbed his eyes, and looked round the room—the room where as a boy he had spent idle hours, where as a student he had been in the hands of his tutor, and as a young man had found recreations such as belong to ambitious and ardent youth. Every corner was familiar. Nothing was changed. The books upon the shelves were as they were placed twenty years ago. And yet he did not seem a part of it. It did not seem natural to him. He was in an atmosphere of strangeness—that atmosphere which surrounds a man, as by a cloud, when some crisis comes upon him and his life seems to stand still, whirling upon its narrow base, while the world appears at an interminable distance, even as to a deaf man who sees yet cannot hear.

There came home to him at that moment with a force indescribable the shamelessness of the act he committed four years ago. He had thought to come back to miserable humiliation. For four years he had refused to do his duty as a man towards an innocent woman,—a woman, though in part a savage,—now transformed into a gentle, noble creature of delight and goodness. How had he deserved it? He had sown the storm, it was but just that he should reap the whirlwind; he had scattered thistles, could he expect to gather grapes? He knew that the sympathy of all his father's house was not with him, but with the woman he had wronged. He was glad it was so. Looking back now, it seemed so poor and paltry a thing that he, a man, should stoop to revenge himself upon those who had given him birth, as a kind of insult to the woman who had lightly set him aside, and should use for that purpose a helpless, confiding girl. To revenge one's self for wrong to one's self is but a common passion, which has little dignity; to avenge some one whom one has loved, man or woman,—and, before all, woman, —has some touch of nobility, is redeemed by loyalty. For his act there was not one word of defence to be made, and he was not prepared to make it.

The cigars and liquors were beside him, but he did not touch them. He seemed very far away from the ordinary details of his life: he knew he had before him hard travel, and he was not confident of the end. He could not tell how long he sat there. After a time the ticking of the clock seemed painfully loud to him. Now and again he heard a cab rattling through the Square, and the foolish song of some drunken loiterer in the night caused him to start painfully. Everything jarred on him. Once he got

up, went to the window, and looked out. The
moon was shining full on the Square. He
wondered if it would be well for him to go out
and find some quiet to his nerves in walking.
He did so. Out in the Square he looked up to
his wife's window. It was lighted. Long time
he walked up and down, his eyes on the window.
It held him like a charm. Once he leaned
against the iron railings of the garden and
looked up, not moving for a time. Presently
he saw the curtain of the window raised, and
against the dim light of the room was outlined
the figure of his wife. He knew it. She stood
for a moment looking out into the night. She
could not see him, nor could he see her features
at all plainly, but he knew that she, like him,
was alone with the catastrophe which his
wickedness had sent upon her. Soon the
curtain was drawn down again, and then he
went once more to the house and took his old
seat beside the table. He fell to brooding, and
at last, exhausted, dropped to a troubled sleep.

He woke with a start. Some one was in the
room. He heard a step behind him. He came
to his feet quickly, a wild light in his eyes. He
faced his brother Richard.

Late in the afternoon Marion had telegraphed
to Richard that Frank was coming. He had
been away visiting some poor and sick people,

and when he came back to Greyhope it was too late to catch the train. But the horses were harnessed straightway, and he was driven into town, a three-hours' drive. He had left the horses at the stables, and, having a latch-key, had come in quietly. He had seen the light in the study, and guessed who was there. He entered, and saw his brother asleep. He watched him for a moment and studied him. Then he moved away to take off his hat, and, as he did so, stumbled slightly. Then it was Frank waked, and for the first time in five years they looked each other in the eyes. They both stood immovable for a moment, and then Richard caught Frank's hand in both of his and said, "God bless you, my boy! I am glad you are back."

"Dick! Dick!" was the reply, and Frank's other hand clutched Richard's shoulder in his strong emotion. They stood silent for a moment longer, and then Richard recovered himself. He waved his hand to the chairs. The strain of the situation was a little painful for them both. Men are shy with each other where their emotions are in play.

"Why, my boy," he said, waving a hand to the wine and liquors, "full bottles and unopened boxes? Tut, tut! here's a pretty how-d'ye-do. Is this the way you toast the home quarters? You're a fine soldier for an old mess!"

So saying, he poured out some whisky, then opened the box of cigars and pushed them towards his brother. He did not care particularly to drink or smoke himself, but a man—an Englishman—is a strange creature. He is most natural and at ease when he is engaged in eating and drinking. He relieves every trying situation by some frivolous and selfish occupation, as of dismembering a partridge, or mixing a punch.

"Well, Frank," said his brother, "now what have you to say for yourself? Why didn't you come long ago? You have played the adventurer for five years, and what have you to show for it? Have you a fortune?" Frank shook his head, and twisted a shoulder. "What have you done that is worth the doing, then?"

"Nothing that I intended to do, Dick," was the grave reply.

"Yes, I imagined that. You have seen *them*, have you, Frank?" he added, in a softer voice.

Frank blew a great cloud of smoke about his face, and through it he said, "Yes, Dick, I have seen a damned sight more than I deserved to see."

"Oh, of course; I know that, my boy; but, so far as I can see, in another direction you are getting quite what you deserve: your wife and child are upstairs; you are here."

158

He paused, was silent for a moment, then leaned over, caught his brother's arm, and said, in a low, strenuous voice, " Frank Armour, you laid a hateful little plot for us. It wasn't manly, but we forgave it and did the best we could. But see here, Frank, take my word for it, you have had a lot of luck; there isn't one woman out of ten thousand that would have stood the test as your wife has stood it ; injured at the start, constant neglect, temptation "——— he paused. " My boy, did you ever think of that, of the temptation to a woman neglected by her husband ? The temptation to men ? Yes, you have had a lot of luck. There has been a special providence for you, my boy; but not for your sake. God doesn't love neglectful husbands, but I think He is pretty sorry for neglected wives."

Frank was very still. His head drooped, the cigar hung unheeded in his fingers for a moment, and he said at last, " Dick, old comrade, I've thought it all over to-night since I came back—everything that you've said. I have not a word of defence to make, but, by heaven ! I'm going to win my wife's love if I can, and when I do it I'll make up for all my cursed foolishness —see if I don't."

" That sounds well, Frank," was the quiet reply. " I like to hear you talk that way. You would be very foolish if you did not. What do you think of the child?"

"Can you ask me what I think? He is a splendid little fellow."

"Take care of him, then,—take good care of him: you may never have another," was the grim rejoinder.

Frank winced. His brother rose, took his arm, and said, "Let us go to our rooms, Frank. There will be time enough to talk later, and I am not so young as I once was."

Truth to say, Richard Armour was not so young as he seemed a few months before. His shoulders were a little stooped, he was greyer about the temples. The little bit of cynicism which had appeared in that remark about the care of the child showed also in the lines of his mouth; yet his eyes had the same old true, honest look. But a man cannot be hit in mortal places once or twice in his life without its being etched on his face or dropped like a pinch of aloe from his tongue.

Still they sat and talked much longer, Frank showing better than when his brother came, Richard gone grey and tired. At last Richard rose and motioned towards the window. "See, Frank," he said, "it is morning." Then he went and lifted the blind. The grey, unpurged air oozed on the glass. The light was breaking over the tops of the houses. A crossing-sweeper early to his task, or holding the key of the street, went pottering by, and a policeman glanced up at them as he passed. Richard drew down the curtain again.

"Dick," said Frank suddenly, "you look old. I wonder if I have changed as much?"

Six months before, Frank Armour would have said that his brother looked young.

"Oh, you look young enough, Frank," was the reply. "But I am a good deal older than I was five years ago. . . . Come, let us go to bed."

# CHAPTER X

AND Lali? How had the night gone for her?
When she rose from the child's cot, where her
lips had caught the warmth that her husband
had left on them, she stood for a moment
bewildered in the middle of the room. She
looked at the door out of which he had gone,
her bosom beating hard, her heart throbbing
so that it hurt her—that she could have cried
out from mere physical pain. The wifedom
in her was plundering the wild stores of her
generous soul for the man, for—as Richard had
said that day, that memorable day!—the father
of her child. But the woman, the pure translated woman, who was born anew when this
frail life in its pink and white glory crept
out into the dazzling world, shrank back, as any
girl might shrink that had not known marriage.
This child had come — from what? She

162

shuddered now—how many times had she done so since she first waked to the vulgar sacrilege of her marriage? She knew now that every good mother, when her first child is born, takes it in her arms, and, all her agony gone, and the ineffable peace of delivered motherhood come, speaks the name of its father, and calls it his child. But—she remembered it now—when her child was born, this little waif, the fruit of a man's hot, malicious hour, she wrapped it in her arms, pressed its delicate flesh to the silken folds of her bosom, and weeping, whispered only, " My child ! my little, little child !"

She had never, as many a wife far from her husband has done, talked to her child of its father, told it of his beauty and his virtues, arrayed it day by day in sweet linen and pretty adornments, as if he were just then knocking at her door ; she had never imagined what he would say when he did come. What could such a father think of his child, born of a woman whose very life he had intended as an insult? No, she had loved it for father and mother also. She had tried to be good, a good mother, living a life unutterably lonely, hard in all that it involved of study, new duty, translation, and burial of primitive emotions. And with all the care and tearful watchfulness that had been needed, she had grown so proud, so exacting—exacting for her child, proud for herself.

How could she know now that this hasty declaration of affection was anything more than the mere man in him? Years ago she had not been able to judge between love and insult— what guarantee had she here? Did he think that she could believe in him?· She was not the woman he had married, he was not the man she had married. He had deceived her basely —she had been a common chattel. She had been miserable enough—could she give herself over to his flying emotions again so suddenly?

She paced the room, her face now in her hands, her hands now clasping and wringing before her. Her wifely duty! She straightened to that. Duty! She was first and before all a good, unpolluted woman. No, no, it could not be. Love him? Again she shrank. Then came flooding on her that afternoon when she had flung herself on Richard's breast, and all those hundred days of happiness in Richard's company—Richard the considerate, the strong, who had stood so by his honour in an hour of peril.

Now as she thought of it a hot wave shivered through all her body, and tingled to her hair. Her face again dropped in her hands, and, as on that other day, she knelt beside the cot, and,

164

bursting into tears, said through her sobs, " My baby! my own dear baby! Oh that we could go away—away—and never come back again!"

She did not know how intense her sobs were. They waked the child from its delicate sleep; its blue eyes opened wide and wise all on the instant, its round soft arm ran up to its mother's neck, and it said, "Don't c'y! I want to s'eep wif you! I'se so s'eepy!"

She caught the child to her wet face, smiled at it through her tears, went with it to her own bed, put it away in the deep whiteness, kissed it, and fondled it away again into the heaven of sleep. When this was done she felt calmer. How she hungered over it! This—this could not be denied her. This, at least, was all hers, without clause or reservation, an absolute love, and an absolute right.

She disrobed and drew in beside the child, and its little dewy cheek touching her breast seemed to ease the ache in her soul.

But sleep would not come. All the past four years trooped by, with their thousand incidents magnified in the sharp, throbbing light of her mind, and at last she knew and saw clearly what was before her, what trials, what duty, and what honour demanded—her honour.

Richard? Once for all she gently put him away from her into that infinite distance of fine respect which a good woman can feel, who has known what she and Richard had known—and set aside. But he had made for her so high a standard, that for one to be measured thereby was a severe challenge.

Could Frank come even to that measure? She dared not try to answer the question. She feared, she shrank, she grew sick at heart. She did not reckon with that other thing, that powerful, infinite influence which ties a woman, she knows not how or why, to the man who led her to the world of motherhood. Through all the wrongs which she may suffer by him, there runs this cable of unhappy attraction, testified to by how many sorrowful lives!

But Lali was trying to think it out, not only to feel, and she did not count that subterranean force which must play its part in this new situation in her drama of life. Could she love him? She crept away out of the haven where her child was, put on her dressing-gown, went to the window, and looked out upon the night, all unconscious that her husband was looking at her from the Square below. Love him?— Love him?—Love him? Could she? Did he love her? Her eyes wandered over the Square. Nowhere else was there a light, but a chimney-flue was creaking somewhere. It jarred on her so that she shrank. Then all at once she smiled to think how she had changed. Four years ago she could have slept amid the hammers of a foundry. The noise ceased. Her eyes passed from the cloud of trees in the Square to the sky —all stars, and restful deep blue. That—that was the same. How she knew it! Orion and Ashtaroth, and Mars and the Pleiades, and the long trail of the Milky Way. As a little child hanging in the trees, or sprawled beside a tepee, she had made friends with them all, even as she learned and loved all the signs of the earth beneath—the twist of a blade of grass, the portent in the cry of a river-hen, the colour of a star, the smell of a wind. She had known Nature then, now she knew men. And knowing them, and having suffered, and sick at heart as she was, standing by this window in the dead of night, the cry that shook her softly was not of her new life, but of the old, primitive, child-like.

*Pasagathe, omarki kethose kolokani, vorgantha pestorondikat Oni.*

"*A spear hath pierced me, and the smart of the nettle is in my wound. Maker of the soft night, bind my wounds with sleep, lest I cry out and be a coward and unworthy.*"

Again and again, unconsciously, the words passed from her lips—

*Vorganthe, pestorondikat Oni.*

167

At last she let down the blind, came to the bed, and once more gathered her child in her arms with an infinite hunger. This love was hers—rich, untrammelled, and so sacred. No matter what came, and she did not know what would come, she had the child. There was a kind of ecstasy in it, and she lay and trembled with the feeling, but at last fell into a troubled sleep.

She waked suddenly to hear footsteps passing her door. She listened. One footstep was heavier than the other—heavier and a little stumbling; she recognised them, Frank and Richard. In that moment her heart hardened. Frank Armour must tread a difficult road.

# CHAPTER XI

FRANK visited the child in the morning, and was received with a casual interest. Richard Joseph Armour was fastidious, was not to be won at the grand gallop. Besides, he had just had a visit from his uncle, and the good taste of that gay time was yet in his mouth. He did not resent the embraces, but he did not respond to them, and he straightened himself with relief when the assault was over. Some one was paying homage to him, that was all he knew; but for his own satisfaction and pleasure he preferred as yet his old comrades, Edward Lambert, Captain Vidall, General Armour, and, above all, Richard. He only showed real interest at the last, when he asked, as it were in compromise, if his father would give him a sword. No one had ever talked to him of his father, and he had no instinct for him so far as could be seen. The sword was, therefore, after the manner of a

169

concession. Frank rashly promised it, and was promptly told by Marion that it couldn't be; and she was backed by Captain Vidall, who said it had already been tabooed, and Frank wasn't to come in and ask for favours or expect them.

The husband and wife met at breakfast. He was down first. When his wife 'entered, he came to her, they touched hands, and she presently took a seat beside him. More than once he paused suddenly in his eating, when he thought of his inexplicable case. He was now face to face with a reversed situation. He had once picked up a pebble from the brown dirt of a prairie, that he might toss it into the pool of this home life; and he had tossed it, and from the sweet bath there had come out a precious stone, which he longed to wear, and knew that he could not—not yet. He could have coerced a lower being, but for his manhood's sake—he had risen to that now, it is curious how the dignity of fatherhood helps to make a man—he could not coerce here, and if he did, he knew that the product would be disaster.

He listened to her talk with Marion and Captain Vidall. Her voice was musical, balanced, her language breathed; it had manner, and an indescribable cadence of intelligence, joined to a deliberation, which touched her off with distinction. When she spoke to him—and she seemed to do that as by studied intention and with tact at certain intervals—her manner was composed and kind. She had resolved on her part. She asked him about his journey over, about his plans for the day, and if he had decided to ride with her in the Park,—he could have the general's mount, she was sure, for the general was not going that day,—and would he mind doing a little errand for her afterwards in Regent Street, for the child,—she feared she herself would not have time?

Just then General Armour entered, and, passing behind her, kissed her on the cheek, dropping his hand on Frank's shoulder at the same time with a hearty greeting. Of course, Frank could have his mount, he said. Mrs. Armour did not come down, but she sent word by Richard, who entered last, that she would be glad to see Frank for a moment before he left for the Park. As of old, Richard took both Lali's hands in his, patted them, and cheerily said—

"Well, well, Lali, we've got the wild man home again safe and sound, haven't we?—the same old vagabond! We'll have to turn him into a Christian again—'for while the lamp holds out to burn '"—

He did not give her time to reply, but their eyes met honestly, kindly, and from the look

they both passed into life and time again with
a fresh courage. She did not know, nor did he,
how near they had been to an abyss; and
neither ever knew. One furtive glance at the
moment, one hesitating pressure of the hand,
one movement of the head from each other's
gaze, and there had been unhappiness for them
all. But they were safe.                     ·

In the Park, Frank and his wife talked little.
They met many who greeted them cordially,
and numbers of Frank's old club friends summoned him to the sacred fires at his earliest
opportunity. The two talked chiefly ot the
people they met, and Frank thrilled with
admiration at his wife's gentle judgment of
everybody.

"The true thing, absolutely the true thing,"
he said; and he was conscious, too, that her
instincts were right and searching, for once or
twice he saw her face chill a little when they
met one or two men whose reputations as
*chevaliers des dames* were pronounced. These
men had had one or two confusing minutes with
Lali in their time.

"How splendidly you ride!" he said, as he
came up swiftly to her, after having chatted for
a moment with Edward Lambert. "You sit
like wax, and so entirely easy."

"Thank you," she said. "I suppose I really

172

like it too well to ride badly, and then I began young on horses not so good as Musket here—bareback, too!" she added, with a little soft irony.

He thought—she did not, however—that she was referring to that first letter he sent home to his people, when he consigned her, like any other awkward freight, to their care. He flushed to his eyes. It cut him deep, but her eyes only had a distant, dreamy look which conveyed nothing of the sting in her words. Like most men, he had a touch of vanity too, and he might have resented the words vaguely, had he not remembered his talk with his mother an hour before.

She had begged him to have patience, she had made him promise that he would not in any circumstance say an ungentle or bitter thing, that he would bide the effort of constant devotion, and his love of the child. Especially must he try to reach her through love of the child.

By which it will be seen that Mrs. Armour had come to some wisdom by reason of her love for Frank's wife and child.

"My son," she had said, "through the child is the surest way, believe me ; for only a mother can understand what that means, how much and how far it goes. You are a father, but

173

until last night you never had the flush of that
love in your veins. You stand yet only at the
door of that life which has done more to guide,
save, instruct, and deepen your wife's life than
anything else, though your brother Richard—
to whom you owe a debt that you can never
repay—has done much indeed. Be wise, my
dear, as I have learned a little to be, since first
your wife came. All might easily have gone
wrong, it has all gone well; and we, my son,
have tried to do our duty lovingly, consistently,
to dear Lali and the child."

She made him promise that he would wait,
that he would not try to hurry his wife's affection for him by any spoken or insistent claim.
"For, Frank dear," she said, "you are only
legally married, not morally, not as God can
bless—not yet. But I pray that what will
sanctify all may come soon, very soon, to the
joy of us all. But again—and I cannot say it
too prayerfully—do not force one little claim
that your marriage gave you, but prove yourself
to her, who has cause to distrust you so much.
Will you forgive your mother, my dear, for
speaking to you?"

He had told her then that what she had
asked he had intended as his own course, yet
what she had said would keep it in his mind
always, for he was sure it was right. Mrs.

Armour had then embraced him, and they
parted. Dealing with Lali had taught them all
much of the human heart that they had never
known before, and the result thereof was wisdom.

They talked casually enough for the rest of
the ride, and before they parted at the door
Frank received his commission for Regent Street,
and accepted it with delight, as a schoolboy
might a gift. He was absurdly grateful for any
favours from her, any sign of her companion-
ship. They met at luncheon ; then, because
Lali had to keep an engagement in Eaton Square,
they parted again, and Frank and Richard took
a walk, after a long hour with the child, who
still so hungered for his sword that Frank
disobeyed orders, and dragged Richard off to
Oxford Street to get one. He was reduced to
a beatific attitude of submission, for he knew
that he had few odds with him now, and that
he must live by virtue of new virtues. He was
no longer proud of himself in any way, and he
knew that no one else was, or rather, he felt so,
and that was just the same.

He talked of the boy, he talked of his wife,
he laid plans, he tore them down, he built them
up again, he asked advice, he did not wait to
hear it, but rambled on, excited, eager. Truth
is, there had suddenly been lifted from his mind
the dread and shadow of four years. Wherever

he had gone, whatever he had been or done, that dread shadow had followed him, and now to know that instead of having to endure a hell he had to win a heaven, and to feel as if his brain had been opened and a mass of vapours and naughty little mannikins of remorse had been let out, was a trifle intoxicating even to a man of his usual vigour and early acquaintance with exciting things.

" Dick, Dick!" he said enthusiastically, "you've been royal. You always were better than any chap I ever knew. You're always doing for others. Hang it, Dick, where does your fun come in? Nobody seems ever to do anything for you."

Richard gave his arm a squeeze. "Never mind about me, boy. I've had all the fun I want, and all I'm likely to get, and so long as you're all willing to have me around, I'm satisfied. There's always a lot to do among the people in the village, one way and another, and I've a heap of reading on, and what more does a fellow want?"

"You didn't always feel that way, Dick?"

"No. You see, at different times in life you want different kinds of pleasures. I've had a good many kinds, and the present kind is about as satisfactory as any."

"But, Dick, you ought to get married. You've

got coin, you've got sense, you're a bit dis-
tinguished-looking, and I'll back your heart
against a thousand bishops. You've never been
in danger of making a fool of yourself as I have.
Why didn't you—why don't you—get married?"

Richard patted his brother's shoulder.

"Married, boy? Married? I've got too much
on my hands. I've got to bring you up yet.
And when that's done I shall have to write a
book called 'How to bring up a Parent.' Then
I've got to help bring your boy up, as I've
done these last three years and more. I've got
to think of that boy for a long while yet, for I
know him better than you do—and I shall need
some of my coin to carry out my plans."

"God bless you, Dick! Bring me up as you
will, only bring *her* along too ; and as for the
boy, you're far more his father than I am. And
my mother says that it's you that's given me the
wife I've got now—so what can I say?—what
can I say?"

It was the middle of the Green Park, and
Richard turned and clasped Frank by both
shoulders.

"Say? Say that you'll stand by the thing
you swore to one mad day in the West as
well as any man that ever lived—'to have and
to hold, to love and to cherish from this day
forth till death us do part, Amen.'"

M                    177

Richard's voice was low and full of a strange, searching something.

Frank, wondering at this great affection and fondness of his brother, looked him in the eyes warmly, solemnly, and replied, " For richer or for poorer, for better or for worse, in sickness and in health—so help me God, and her kindness and forgiveness!"

# CHAPTER XII

FRANK and Lali did not meet until dinner was announced. The conversation at dinner was mainly upon the return to Greyhope which was fixed for the following morning, and it was deftly kept gay and superficial by Marion and Richard and Captain Vidall, until General Armour became reminiscent, and held the interest of the table through a dozen little incidents of camp and barrack life until the ladies rose. There had been an engagement for late in the evening, but it had been given up because of Frank's home-coming, and there was to be a family gathering merely—for Captain Hume Vidall was now as much one of the family as Frank or Richard, by virtue of his approaching marriage with Marion. The men left alone, General Armour questioned Frank freely about life in the Hudson's Bay country, and the conversation ran on idly till it was time to join the ladies.

179

When they reached the drawing-room, Marion
was seated at the piano, playing a rhapsody of
Raff's, and Mrs. Armour and Lali were seated
side by side.   Frank thrilled at seeing his wife's
hand in his mother's.   Marion nodded over the
piano at the men, and presently played a snatch
of *Carmen*, then wandered off into the barbaric
strength of *Tannhauser*, and as suddenly again
into the ballet music of *Faust*.

"Why so wilful, my girl?" said her father,
who had a keen taste for music.   "Why this
tangle?   Let us have something definite."

Marion sprang up from the piano.   "I can't.
I'm not definite myself to-night."   Then, turning
to Lali, "Lali dear, sing something—do! sing
my favourite, 'The Chase of the Yellow Swan.'"

This was a song which in the later days at
Greyhope, Lali had sung for Marion, first in her
own language, with the few notes of an Indian
chant, and afterwards, by the help of the cele-
brated musician who had taught her both music
and singing, both of which she had learned but
slowly, it was translated and set to music.   Lali
looked Marion steadily in the eyes for a moment,
and then rose.   It cost her something to do this
thing, for while she had often talked much and
long with Richard about that old life, it now
seemed as if she were to sing it to one who
would not quite understand why she should sing

it at all, or what was her real attitude towards
her past—that she looked upon it from the
infinite distance of affectionate pity, knowledge,
and indescribable change, and yet loved the
inspiring atmosphere and mystery of that lonely
North, which once in the veins never leaves it—
never. Would *he* understand that she was feeling, not the common detail of the lodge and the
camp-fire and the Company's post, but the deep
spirit of Nature, filtering through the senses in a
thousand ways—the wild ducks' flight, the sweet
smell of the balsam, the exquisite gallop of the
deer, the powder of the frost, the sun and snow
and blue plains of water, the thrilling eternity of
plain and the splendid steps of the hills, which
led away by stair and entresol to the Kimash
Hills, the Hills of the Mighty Men?

She did not know what he would think, and
again on second thought she determined to make
him, by this song, contrast her as she was when
he married her, and now—how she herself could
look upon that past unabashed, speak of it without blushing, sing of it with pride, having reached
a point where she could look down and say,
"This was the way by which I came."

She rose, and was accompanied to the piano
by General Armour, Frank admiring her soft,
springing steps, her figure so girlish and lissom.
She paused for a little before she began.

Her eyes showed for a moment over the piano, deep, burning, inlooking ; then they veiled ; her fingers touched the keys, wandered over them in a few strange, soft chords, paused, wandered again, more firmly and very intimately, and then she sang. Her voice was a good contralto, well-balanced, true, of no great range, but within its compass melodious, and having some inexpressible charm of temperament. Frank did not need to strain his ears to hear the words ; every one came clear, searching, delicately valued—

In the flash of the singing dawn,
At the door of the Great One,
The joy of his lodge knelt down,
Knelt down, and her hair in the sun
Shone like showering dust,
And her eyes were as eyes of the fawn.
And she cried to her lord,
" O my lord, O my life,
From the desert I come ;
From the hills of the Dawn."
And he lifted the curtain and said,
" Hast thou seen It, the Yellow Swan ?"

And she lifted her head, and her eyes
Were as lights in the dark,
And her hands folded slow on her breast,
And her face was as one who has seen
The gods and the place where they dwell ;
And she said, " Is it meet that I kneel,
That I kneel as I speak to my lord ?"

And he answered her, "Nay, but to stand,
And to sit by my side ;
But speak, thou hast followed the trail,
Hast thou found It, the Yellow Swan?"

And she stood as a queen, and her voice
Was as one who hath seen the Hills,
The Hills of the Mighty Men,
And hath heard them cry in the night,
Hath heard them call in the dawn,
Hath seen It, the Yellow Swan.
And she said, "It is not for my lord ;"
And she murmured, "I cannot tell,
But my lord must go as I went,
And my lord must come as I came,
And my lord shall be wise !"

And he cried in his wrath,
" What is thine, it is mine,
And thine eyes are my eyes,
Thou shalt speak of the Yellow Swan !"
But she answered him, "Nay, though I die.
I have lain in the nest of the Swan,
I have heard, I have known ;
When thine eyes too have seen,
When thine ears too have heard,
Thou shalt do with me then as thou wilt !"

And he lifted his hand to strike,
And he straightened his spear to slay,
But a great light struck on his eyes,
And he heard the rushing of wings,
And his long spear fell from his hand,
And a terrible stillness came.
And when the spell passed from his eyes,
He stood in his doorway alone,
And gone was the queen of his soul,
And gone was the Yellow Swan.

Frank Armour listened as in a dream. The song had the wild swing of savage life, the deep sweetness of a monotone, but it had also the fine intelligence, the subtle allusiveness of romance. He could read between the lines. The allegory touched him where his nerves were sensitive. Where she had gone he could not go until his eyes had seen and known what hers had seen and known; he could not grasp his happiness all in a moment; she was no longer at his feet, but equal with him, and wiser than he. She had not meant the song to be allusive when she began, but to speak to him through it by singing the heathen song as his own sister might sing it. As the song went on, however, she felt the inherent suggestion in it, so that when she had finished it required all her strength to get up calmly, come among them again, and listen to their praises and thanks. She had no particular wish to be alone with Frank just yet, but the others soon arranged themselves so that the husband and wife were left in a cosy corner of the room.

Lali's heart fluttered a little at first, for the day had been trying, and she was not as strong as she could wish. Admirably as she had gone through the season, it had worn on her, and her constitution had become sensitive and delicate, while yet strong. The life had almost refined

184

her too much. Always on the watch that she should do exactly as Marion or Mrs. Armour, always so sensitive as to what was required of her, always preparing for this very time, now that it had come, and her heart and mind were strong, her body seemed to weaken. Once or twice during the day she had felt a little faint, but it had passed off, and she had scolded herself. She did not wish a serious talk with her husband to-night, but she saw now that it was inevitable.

He said to her as he sat down beside her, "You sing very well indeed. The song is full of meaning, and you bring it all out."

"I am glad you like it," she responded conventionally; "of course it's an unusual song for an English drawing-room."

"As you sing it, it would be beautiful and acceptable anywhere, Lali."

"Thank you again," she answered, closing and unclosing her fan, her eyes wandering to where Mrs. Armour was. She wished she could escape, for she did not feel like talking, and yet though the man was her husband she could not say that she was too tired to talk ; she must be polite. Then, with a little dainty malice, "It is more interesting, though, in the vernacular—and costume!"

"Not unless you sang it so," he answered gallantly, and with a kind of earnestness.

"You have not forgotten the way of London men," she rejoined.

"Perhaps that is well, for I do not know the way of women," he said, with a faint bitterness. "Yet I don't speak unadvisedly in this,"—here he meant to be a little bold, and bring the talk to the past,—"for I heard you sing that song once before."

She turned on him half puzzled, a little nervous. "Where did you hear me sing it?"

He had made up his mind, wisely enough, to speak with much openness and some tact also, if possible.

"It was on the Glow Worm River at the Clip Claw Hills. I came into your father's camp one evening in the autumn, hungry and tired and knocked about. I was given the next tent to yours. It was night, and just before I turned in I heard your voice singing. I couldn't understand much of the language, but I had the sense of it, and I know it when I hear it again."

"Yes, I remember singing it that night," she said. "Next day was the Feast of the Yellow Swan."

Her eyes presently became dreamy, and her face took on a distant, rapt look. She sat looking straight before her for a moment.

He did not speak, for he interpreted the look aright, and he was going to be patient, to wait.

186

"Tell me of my father," she said. "You have been kind to him?"

He winced a little. "When I left Fort Charles he was very well," he said, "and he asked me to tell you to come some day. He also has sent you a half-dozen silver fox skins, a sash, and moccasins made by his own hands. The things are not yet unpacked."

Moccasins? She remembered when last she had moccasins on her feet—the day she rode the horse at the quick-set hedge, and nearly lost her life. How very distant that all was, and yet how near too! Suddenly she remembered also why she took that mad ride, and her heart hardened a little.

"You have been kind to my father since I left?" she asked.

He met her eyes steadily. "No, not always; not more than I have been kind to you. But at the last, yes." Suddenly his voice became intensely direct and honest. "Lali," he continued, "there is much that I want to say to you." She waved her hand in a wearied fashion. "I want to tell you that I would do the hardest penance if I could wipe out these last four years."

"Penance?" she said dreamily,—"penance? What guarantee of happiness would that be? One would not wish another to do penance if"— She paused.

187

"I understand," he said,—"if one cared—if one loved. Yes, I understand. But that does not alter the force or meaning of the wish. I swear to you that I repent with all my heart— the first wrong to you, the long absence—the neglect—everything."

She turned slowly to him. "Everything?— Everything?" she repeated after him. "Do you understand what that means? Do you know a woman's heart? No. Do you know what a shameful neglect is at the most pitiful time in your life? No. How can a man know? He has a thousand things—the woman has nothing, nothing at all except the refuge of home, that for which she gave up everything!"

Presently she broke off, and something sprang up and caught her in the throat. Years of indignation were at work in her. "I have had a home," she said, in a low, thrilling voice,—"a good home; but what did that cost you? Not one honest sentiment of pity, kindness, or solici- tude. You clothed me, fed me, abandoned me, as—how can one say it? Do I not know, if coming back you had found me as you expected to find me, what the result would have been? Do I not know? You would have endured me if I did not thrust myself upon you, for you have after all a sense of legal duty, a kind of stubborn honour. But you would have

made my life such that some day one or both of
us would have died suddenly. For "—she looked
him with a hot clearness in the eyes—"for
there is just so much that a woman can bear.
I wish this talk had not come now, but, since it
has come, it is better to speak plainly. You see,
you misunderstand. A heathen has a heart as
another—has a life to be spoiled or made happy
as another. Had there been one honest passion
in your treatment of me—in your marrying me—
there would be something on which to base
mutual respect, which is more or less necessary
when one is expected to love. But—but I will
not speak more of it, for it chokes me, the insult
to me, not as I was, but as I am. Then it would
probably have driven me mad, if I had known;
now it eats into my life like rust!"

He made a motion as if to take her hands,
but lifting them away quietly she said, "You
forget that there are others present, as well as
the fact that we can talk better without demon-
strations."

He was about to speak, but she stopped him.
"No, wait," she said; "for I want to say a little
more. I was only an Indian girl, but you must
remember that I had also in my veins good
white blood, Scotch blood. Perhaps it was that
which drew me to you then—for Lali the Indian
girl loved you. Life had been to me pleasant

189

enough—without care, without misery, open, strong, and free ; our people were not as those others which had learned the white man's vices. We loved the hunt, the camp-fires, the sacred feasts, the legends of the Mighty Men ; and the earth was a good friend, whom we knew as the child knows its mother."

She paused. Something seemed to arrest her attention. Frank followed her eyes. She was watching Captain Vidall and Marion. He guessed what she was thinking—how different her own wooing had been from theirs, how concerning her courtship she had not one sweet memory—the thing that keeps alive more love and loyalty in this world than anything else. Presently General Armour joined them, and Frank's opportunity was over for the present.

Captain Vidall and Marion were engaged in a very earnest conversation, though it might not appear so to observers.

"Come now, Marion," he said protestingly, "don't be impossible. Please give the day a name. Don't you think we've waited about long enough ? "

"There was a man in the Bible who served seven years."

"I've served over three in India since I met you at the well, and that counts double. Why so particular to a day?—it's a bit Jewish.

Anyhow, that seven years was rough on Rachel."

"How, Hume? Because she got *passée*?"

"Well, that counted; but do you suppose that Jew was going to put in those seven years without interest? Don't you believe it. Rachel paid capital and interest back, or Jacob was no Jew. Tell me, Marion, when shall it be?"

"Hume, for a man who has trifled away years in India, you are strangely impatient."

"Mrs. Lambert says that I have the sweetest disposition."

"My *dear* sir!"

"Don't look at me like that at this distance, or I shall have to wear goggles, as the man did who went courting the Sun."

"How supremely ridiculous you are! And I thought you such a sensible, serious man."

"Mrs. Lambert put that in your head. We used to meet at the annual dinners of the Bible Society."

"Why do you tell me such stuff?"

"It's a fact. Her father and my aunt were in that swim, and we were sympathisers."

"Mercenary people!"

"It worked very well in her case; not so well in mine. But we conceived a profound respect for each other then. But tell me, Marion, when is it to be? Why put off the inevitable?"

"It isn't inevitable—and I'm only twenty-three."

" Only twenty-three,
And as good fish in the sea "—

he responded, laughing. "Yes, but you've set the precedent for a courtship of four years and a bit, and what man could face it?"

"You did."

"Yes, but I wasn't advertised of the fact beforehand. Suppose I had seen the notice at the start, 'This mortgage cannot be raised inside of four years—and a bit!' There's a limit to human endurance."

"Why shouldn't I hold to the number, but alter the years to days?"

"You wouldn't dare. A woman must live up to her reputation."

"Indeed? What an ambition!"

"And a man to his manners."

"An unknown quantity."

"And a lover to his promises."

"A book of jokes." Marion had developed a taste for satire.

"Which reminds me of Lady Halwood and Mrs. Lambert. Lady Halwood was more impertinent than usual the other day at the Sinclairs' show, and had a little fling at Mrs. Lambert. The talk turned on gowns. Lady Halwood was much interested at once. She has a weakness that way. 'Why,' said she, 'I like these fashions this year, but I'm not sure that they suit me. They're the same as when the Queen came to the throne.' 'Well,' said Mrs. Lambert sweetly, 'if they suited you then'— There was an audible titter, and Mrs. Lambert had an enemy for life."

"I don't see the point of your story in this connection."

"No? Well, it was merely to suggest that if you had to live up to this scheme of four-years' probation, other people besides lovers would make up books of jokes, and"—

"That's like a man—to threaten."

"Yes, I threaten—on my knees."

"Hume, how long do you think Frank will have to wait?"

They were sitting where they had a good view of the husband and wife, and Vidall, after a moment, said—

"I don't know. She has waited four years too ; now it looks as if, like Jacob, she was going to gather in her shekels of interest compounded."

"It isn't going to be a bit pleasant to watch."

"But you won't be here to see."

Marion ignored the suggestion. "She seems to have hardened since he came yesterday. I

N            193

hardly know her ; and yet she looks awfully worn to-night, don't you think ? "

" Yes, as if she had to keep a hand on herself. But it'll come out all right in the end, you'll see."

" Yes, of course ; but she might be sensible and fall in love with Frank at once. That's what she did when "—

" When she didn't know man."

" Yes, but where would you all be if we women acted on what we know of you ? "

" On our knees chiefly, as I am. Remember this, Marion, that half a sinner is better than no man."

" You mean that no man is better than half a saint ? "

" How you must admire me ! "

" Why ? "

" As you are about to name the day, I assume that I'm a whole saint in your eyes."

" St. Augustine ! "

" Who was he ? "

" A man that reformed."

" Before or after marriage ? "

" Before, I suppose."

" I don't think he died happy."

' Why not ? "

" I've a faint recollection that he was boiled."

"Don't be horrid. What has that to do with it?"

"Nothing, perhaps. But he probably broke out again after marriage, and sank at last into that cauldron. That's what it means by being —steeped in crime."

"How utterly nonsensical you are!"

"I feel light-headed. You've been at sea, on a yacht becalmed, haven't you? when along comes a ground-swell, and as you rock in the sun there comes trouble, and your head goes round like a top? Now, that's my case. I've been becalmed four years, and while I pray for a little wind to take me—home, you rock me in the trough of uncertainty. Suspense is very gall and wormwood. You know what the jailer said to the criminal who was hanging on a reprieve, 'Rope deferred maketh the heart sick.' Marion, give me the hour, or give me the rope."

"The rope enough to hang yourself?"

She suddenly reached up and pulled a hair from her head. She laid it in his hand—a long brown silken thread. "Hume," she said airily yet gently, "there is the rope. Can you love me for a month of Sundays?"

"Yes, for ever and a day!"

"I will cancel the day, and take your bond for the rest. I will be generous. I will marry you in two months—and a day."

"My dearest girl!"—he drew her hand into both of his,—"I can't have you more generous than myself, I'll throw off the month." But his eyes were shining very seriously, though his mouth smiled.

"Two months and a day," she repeated.

"We must all bundle off to Greyhope to-morrow," came General Armour's voice across the room; "down comes the baby, cradle and all."

Lali rose. "I am very tired," she said; "I think I will say good-night."

"I'll go and see the boy with you," Frank said, rising also.

Lali turned towards Marion. Marion's face was flushed, and had a sweet, happy confusion. With a low, trembling good-night to Captain Vidall, a hurried kiss on her mother's cheek, and a tiptoed caress on her father's head, she ran and linked her arm in Lali's, and together they proceeded to the child's room. Richard was there when they arrived, mending a broken toy. Two hours later, the brothers parted at Frank's door.

"Reaping the whirlwind, Dick?" Frank said, dropping his hand on his brother's arm.

Richard pointed to the child's room.

"Nonsense! Do you want all the world at once? You are reaping the forgiveness of your sins."

Somehow Richard's voice was a little stern.

"I was thinking of my devilry, Dick,—that's the whirlwind—here!" His hand dropped on his breast.

"That's where it ought to be. Good-night."

"Good-night."

# CHAPTER XIII

PART of Frank's most trying interview, next to the meeting with his wife, was that with Mackenzie, who had been his special commissioner in the movement of his masquerade. Mackenzie also had learned a great deal since she had brought Lali—home. She, like others, had come to care truly for the sweet barbarian, and served her with a grim kind of reverence. Just in proportion as this had increased, her respect for Frank had decreased. No man can keep a front of dignity in the face of an unbecoming action. However, Mackenzie had her moment, and when it was over, the new life began at no general disadvantage to Frank. To all save the immediate family Frank and Lali were a companionable husband and wife. She rode with him, occasionally walked with him, now and again sang to him, and they appeared in the streets of St. Albans and at the Abbey together, and oftener still in the village church near, where the Armours of many generations were proclaimed of much account in the solid virtues of tomb and tablet.

The day had gone by when Lali attracted any especial notice among the villagers, and she enjoyed the quiet beauty and earnestness of the service. But she received a shock one Sunday. She had been nervous all the week, she could not tell why, and others remarked how her face had taken on a new sensitiveness, a delicate anxiety, and that her strength was not what it had been. As, for instance, after riding she required to rest, a thing before unknown, and she often lay down for an hour before dinner. Then, too, at table once she grew suddenly pale and swayed against Edward Lambert, who was sitting next to her. She would not, however, leave the table, but sat the dinner out, to Frank's apprehension. He was devoted, but it was clear to Marion and her mother at least that his attentions were trying to her. They seemed to put her under an obligation which to meet was a trial. There is nothing more wearing to a woman than affectionate attentions from a man who has claims upon her, but whom she does not love. These same attentions from one who has no claims give her a thrill of pleasure. It is useless to ask for justice in such a matter. These things are governed by no law ; and rightly so, else the world would be in good time a loveless multitude, held together only by the hungering ties of parent and child.

But this Sunday wherein Lali received a shock. She did not know that the banns for Marion's and Captain Vidall's marriage were to be announced, and at the time her thoughts were far away. She was recalled to herself by the clergyman's voice pronouncing their names, and saying, "*If any of you do know cause or just imp.diment why these two people should not be joined together in the bonds of holy matrimony, ye are to declare it.*" All at once there came back to her her own marriage, when the Protestant missionary, in his nasal monotone, numbled these very words, not as if he expected that any human being would, or could, offer objection.

She almost sprang from her seat now. Her nerves all at once came to such a tension that she could have cried out. Why had there been no one there at her marriage to say, "I forbid it"? How shameful it had all been! And the first kiss her husband had given her had the flavour of brandy! If she could but turn back the hands upon the clock of Time! Under the influence of the music and the excited condition of her nerves, the event became magnified, dis-

200

torted ; it burned into her brain. It was not made less poignant by the sermon from the text, " *Mene, Mene, Tekel, Upharsin.*" When the words were first announced in the original, it sounded like her own language, save that it was softer, and her heart throbbed fast. Then came the interpretation, " *Thou art weighed in the balance and found wanting.*"

Then suddenly swept over her a new feeling, one she had never felt before. Up to this point a determination to justify her child, to reverse the verdict of the world, to turn her husband's sin upon himself, had made her defiant, even bitter ; in all things eager to live up to her new life, to the standard that Richard had by manner and suggestion, rather than by words, laid down for her. But now there came in upon her a flood of despair. At best she was only of this race through one - third of her parentage, and education and refinement and all things could do no more than make her possible. There must always be in the record, " She was of a strange people. She was born in a wigwam." She did not know that failing health was really the cause of this lapse of self-confidence, this growing self-depreciation, this languor for which she could not account. She found that she could not toss the child and frolic with it as she had done ; she was conscious that within a month there had stolen upon her the desire to be much alone, to avoid noises and bustle—it irritated her. She found herself thinking more and more of her father, her father to whom she had never written one line since she had left the North. She had had good reasons for not writing—writing could do no good whatever, particularly to a man who could not read, and who would not have understood her new life if he had read. Yet now she seemed not to know why she had not written, and to blame herself for neglect and forgetfulness. It weighed on her. Why had she ever been taken from the place of tamarack-trees and the sweeping prairie grass? No, no, she was not, after all, fit for this life. She had been mistaken, and Richard had been mistaken— Richard, who was so wise. The London season? Ah! that was because people had found a novelty, and herself of better manners than had been expected.

The house was now full of preparations for the wedding. It stared her in the face every day, almost every hour. Dressmakers, milliners, tailors, and all those other necessary people. Did the others think what all this meant to her? It was impossible that they should. When Marion came back from town at night and told of her trials among the dressmakers,

when she asked the general opinion and sometimes individual judgment, she could not know
that it was at the expense of Lali's nerves.

Lali, when she married, had changed her
moccasins, combed her hair, and put on a fine
red belt, and that was all. She was not envious
now, not at all. But somehow it all was a
deadly kind of evidence against herself and her
marriage. Her reproach was public, the world
knew it, and no woman can forgive a public
shame, even was it brought about by a man she
loved, or loves. Her chiefest property in life is
her self-esteem and her name before the world.
Rob her of these, and her heaven has fallen,
and if a man has shifted the foundations of
her peace, there is no forgiveness for him till
her Paradise has been reconquered. So busy
were all the others that they did not see how
her strength was failing. There were three
weeks between the day the banns were announced and the day of the wedding, which was
to be in the village church, not in town; for, as
Marion said, she had seen too many marriages
for one day's triumph and criticism; she wanted
hers where there would be neither triumph nor
criticism, but among people who had known
her from her childhood up. A happy romance
had raised Marion's point of view.

Meanwhile Frank was winning the confidence

of his own child, who, however, ranked Richard higher always, and became to a degree his father's tyrant. But Frank's nature was undergoing a change. His point of view also had enlarged. The suffering, bitterness, and humiliation of his life in the North had done him good. He was being disciplined to take his position as a husband and father, but he sometimes grew heavy-hearted when he saw how his attentions oppressed his wife, and had it not been for Richard he might probably have brought on disaster, for the position was trying to all concerned. A few days before the wedding Edward Lambert and his wife arrived, and he, Captain Vidall, and Frank Armour took rides and walks together, or set the world right in the billiard-room. Richard seldom joined them, though their efforts to induce him to do so were many. He had his pensioners, his books, his pipe, and "the boy," and he had returned in all respects, in so far as could be seen, to his old life, save for the new and larger interest of his nephew.

One evening the three men with General Armour were all gathered in the billiard-room. Conversation had been general and without particular force, as it always is when merely civic or political matters are under view. But some one gave a social twist to the talk, and

presently they were launched upon that sea
where every man provides his own chart, or he
is a very worm and no man. Each man had
been differently trained, each viewed life from
a different standpoint, and yet each had been
brought up in the same social atmosphere, in
the same social sets, had imbibed the same
traditions, been moved generally by the same
public considerations.

"But there's little to be said for a man who
doesn't, outwardly at least, live up to the social
necessity," said Lambert.

"And keep the Ten Commandments in the
vulgar tongue," rejoined Vidall.

"I've lived seventy odd years, and I've
knocked about a good deal in my time," said
the general, "but I've never found that you
could make a breach of social necessity, as you
call it, without paying for it one way or another.
The trouble with us when we're young is that
we want to get more out of life than there really
is in it. There is not much in it, after all. You
can stand just so much fighting, just so much
work, just so much emotion—and you can stand
less emotion than anything else. I'm sure more
men and women break up from a hydrostatic
pressure of emotion than from anything else.
Upon my soul, that's so."

"You are right, General," said Lambert.

"The steady way is the best way. The world is a passable place if a fellow has a decent income by inheritance, or can earn a big one, but to be really contented to earn money it must be a big one, otherwise he is far better pleased to take the small inherited income. It has a lot of dignity, which the other can only bring when it is large."

"That's only true in this country ; it's not true in America," said Frank, "for there the man who doesn't earn money is looked upon as a muff, and is treated as such. A small inherited income is thought to be a trifle enervating. But there is a country of emotions, if you like. The American heart is worn upon the American sleeve, and the American mind is the most active thing in this world. That's why they grow old so young."

"I met a woman a year or so ago at dinner," said Vidall, "who looked forty. She looked it, and she acted it. She was younger than any woman present, but she seemed older. There was a kind of hopeless languor about her which struck me as pathetic. Yet she had been beautiful, and might even have been so when I saw her, if it hadn't been for that look. It was the look of a person who had no interest in things. And the person who has no interest in things is the person who once had a great

deal of interst in things, who had too passionate
an interest. The revulsion is always terrible.
Too much romance is deadly. It is as false a
stimulant as opium or alcohol, and leaves a
corresponding mark. Well, I heard her history.
She was married at fifteen — ran away to be
married ; and in spite of the fact that a railway
accident nearly took her husband from her on
the night of her marriage — one would have
thought that would make a strong bond—she
was soon alive to the attentions that are given
pretty and—considerate woman. At a ball
at Naples, her husband, having in vain tried to
induce her to go home, picked her up under his
arm and carried her out of the ballroom. Then
came a couple of years of opium-eating, fierce
social excitement, divorce, new marriage, and
so on, until her husband agreeably decided to
live in Nice, while she lived somewhere else.
Four days after I had met her at the dinner I
saw her again. I could scarcely believe my
eyes. The woman had changed completely.
She was young again—twenty-five, in face and
carriage, in the eye and hand, in step and voice."

"Who was the man?" suggested Frank
Armour.

"A man about her own age, or a little more,
but who was an infant beside her in knowledge
of the world."

207

"She was in love with the fellow? It was a *grande passion?*" asked Lambert.

"In love with him? No, not at all. It was a momentary revival of an old—possibility."

"You mean that such women never really love?"

"Perhaps once, Frank, but only after a fashion. The rest was mere imitation of their first impulses."

"And this woman?"

"Well, the end came sooner than I expected. I tell you I was shocked at the look in her face when I saw it again. That light had flickered out; the sensitive alertness of hand, eye, voice, and carriage had died away; lines had settled in the face, and the face itself had gone cold, with that hard, cold passiveness which comes from exhausted emotions and a closed heart. The jewels she wore might have been put upon a statue with equal effect."

"It seems to me that we might pitch into men in these things and not make women the dreadful examples," said a voice from the corner. It was the voice of Richard, who had but just entered.

"My dear Dick," said his father, "men don't make such frightful examples, because these things mean less to men than they do to women. Romance is an incident to a man; he

can even come through an *affaire* with no ideals
gone, with his mental fineness unimpaired ; but
it is different with a woman.   She has more
emotion than mind, else there were no cradles
in the land.   Her standards are set by the
rules of the heart, and when she has broken
these rules she has lost her standard too.   But
to come back, it is true, I think, as I said, that
man or woman must not expect too much out
of life, but be satisfied with what they can get
within the normal courses of society and convention and home, and the end thereof is peace,
—yes, upon my soul, it's peace."

There was something very fine in the blunt,
honest words of the old man, whose name had
ever been sweet with honour.

" And the chief thing is that a man live up to
his own standard," said Lambert.   " Isn't that
so, Dick ?—you're the wise man."

" Every man should have laws of his own, I
should think ; commandments of his own, for
every man has a different set of circumstances
wherein to work—or worry."

" The wisest man I ever knew," said Frank,
dropping his cigar, "was a little French Can-
adian trapper up in the Saskatchewan country.
A priest asked him one day what was the best
thing in life, and he answered, ' For a young
man's mind to be old, and an old man's heart to

O                     209

be young.' The priest asked him how that could be. And he said, 'Good food, a good woman to teach him when he is young, and a child to teach him when he is old.' Then the priest said, 'What about the Church and the love of God?' The little man thought a little, and then said, 'Well, it is the same—the love of man and woman came first in the world, then the child, then God in the garden.' Afterward he made a little speech of good-bye to us, for we were going to the south while he remained in a fork of the Far Off River. It was like some ancient blessing : that we should always have a safe tent and no sorrow as we travelled ; that we should always have a *cache* for our food, and food for our *cache* ; that we should never find a tree that would not give sap, nor a field that would not grow grain ; that our bees should not freeze in winter, and that the honey should be thick, and the comb break like snow in the teeth ; that we keep hearts like the morning, and that we come slow to the Four Corners where man says Good-night."

Each of the other men present wondered at that instant if Frank Armour would, or could, have said this with the same feelings two months before. He seemed almost transformed.

" It reminds me," said the general, "of an inscription from an Egyptian monument which an officer of the First put into English verse for me years ago—

> "Fair be the garden where their loves shall dwell,
> Safe be the highway where their feet may go,
> Rich be the fields wherein their hands may toil,
> The fountains many where their good wines flow.
> Full be their harvest-bins with corn and oil,
> To sorrow may their humour be a foil;
> Quick be their hearts all wise delights to know,
> Fly their footsteps to the gate Farewell."

was a moment's silence after he had finished, and then there was noise without, a sound of pattering feet; the door flew open, and in ran a little figure in white—young Richard in his bedgown, who had broken away from his nurse, and had made his way to the billiard-room, where he knew his uncle had gone.

The child's face was flashing with mischief and adventure. He ran in among the group, and stretched out his hands with a little fighting air. His uncle Richard made a step toward him, but he ran back; his father made as if to take him in his arms, but he evaded him. Presently the door opened, the nurse entered, the child sprang from among the group, and ran with a laughing defiance to the farthest end of the room, and, leaning his chin on the billiard-table, flashed a look of defiant humour at his pursuer. Presently the door opened again, and the figure of the mother appeared. All at once the child's face altered ; he stood perfectly still, and waited for his mother to come to him. Lali had not spoken, and she did not speak until, lifting the child, she came the length of the billiard-table and faced them.

"I beg your pardon," she said, "for intruding; but Richard has led us a dance, and I suppose the mother may go where her child goes."

"The mother and the child are always welcome wherever they go," said General Armour quietly.

All the men had risen to their feet, and they made a kind of semicircle before her. The white-robed child had clasped its arms about her neck, and nestled its face against hers, as if, with perfect satisfaction, it had got to the end of its adventure, but the look of humour was still in the eyes as they ran from Richard to his father and back again.

Frank Armour stepped forward and took the child's hand, as it rested on the mother's shoulder. Lali's face underwent a slight change as her husband's fingers touched her neck.

"I must go," she said. "I hope I have not broken up a serious conversation—or were you not so serious, after all? she said, glancing archly at General Armour.

212

"We were talking of women," said Lambert.
"The subject is wide," replied Lali, "and the speakers many. One would think some wisdom might be got in such a case."

"Believe me, we were not trying to understand the subject," said Captain Vidall; "the most that a mere man can do is to appreciate it."

"There are some things that are hidden from the struggling mind of man, and are revealed unto babes and the mothers of babes," said General Armour gravely, as, reaching out his hands, he took the child from the mother's arms, kissed it full upon the lips, and added, "Men do not understand women, because men's minds have not been trained in the same school. When once a man has mastered the very alphabet of motherhood, then he shall have mastered the mind of woman; but I, at least, refuse to say that I do not understand, from the standpoint of modern cynicism."

"Ah, General, General!" said Lambert, "we have lost the chivalric way of saying things, which belongs to your generation."

By this time the wife had reached the door; she turned and held out her arms for the child. General Armour came and placed the boy where he had found it, and, with eyes suddenly filling, laid both his hands upon Lali's, and they clasped the child, and said, "It is worth while to have lived so long and to have seen so much." Her eyes met his in a wistful, anxious expression, shifted to those of her husband, dropped to the cheeks of the child, and with the whispered word, which no one, not even the general heard, she passed from the room, the nurse following her.

Perhaps some of the most striking contrasts are achieved in the least melodramatic way. The sudden incursion of the child and its mother into the group, the effect of their presence, and their soft departure, leaving behind them, as it were, a trail of light, changed the whole atmosphere of the room, as though some new life had been breathed into it, charged each mind with new sensations, and gave each figure new attitude. Not a man present but had had his full swing with the world, none worse than most men, none better than most, save that each had latent in him a good sense of honour concerning all civic and domestic virtues. They were not men of sentimentality; they were not accustomed to exposing their hearts upon their sleeve, but each, as the door closed, recognised that something for one instant had come in among them, had made their past conversation to appear meagre, crude, and lacking in both height and depth. Somehow, they seemed to feel, although no words expressed the thought, that for an instant they were in the presence of a wisdom greater than any wisdom of a man's smoking-room.

"It is wonderful, wonderful," said the general slowly, and no man asked him why he said it, or what was wonderful. But Richard, sitting apart, watched Frank's face acutely, himself wondering when the hour would come that the wife would forgive her husband, and this situation, so fraught with danger, would be relieved.

# CHAPTER XIV

## ON THE EDGE OF A FUTURE

AT last the day of the wedding came, a beautiful September day, which may be more beautiful in uncertain England than anywhere else. Lali had been strangely quiet all the day before, and she had also seemed strangely delicate. Perhaps, or perhaps not, she felt the crisis was approaching. It is probable that when the mind has been strained for a long time, and the heart and body suffered much, one sees a calamity vaguely, and cannot define it; appreciates it, and does not know it. She came to Marion's room about a half-hour before they were to start for the church. Marion was already dressed and ready, save for the few final touches, which, though they have been given a dozen times, must still again be given just before the bride starts for the church. Such is the anxious mind of women on these occasions. The two stood and looked

at each other a moment, each wondering what
were the thoughts of the other. Lali was struck
by that high, proud look over which lay a
glamour of infinite satisfaction, of sweetness,
which comes to every good woman's face when
she goes to the altar in a marriage which is not
contingent on the rise or fall in stocks, or a
satisfactory settlement. Marion, looking, saw,
as if it had been revealed to her all at once, the
intense and miraculous change which had come
over the young wife, even within the past two
months. Indeed, she had changed as much
within that time as within all the previous four
years—that is, she had been brought to a certain
point in her education and experience, where
without a newer and deeper influence she could
go no further. That newer and deeper influence
had come, and the result thereof was a woman
standing upon the verge of the real tragedy to
her life, which was not in having married the
man, but in facing that marriage with her new
intelligence and a transformed soul. Men can
face that sort of thing with a kind of philosophy, not because men are better or wiser,
but because it really means less to them. They
have resources of life, they can bury themselves
in their ambitions good or bad, but a woman
can only bury herself in her affections, unless
her heart has been closed ; and in that case she

herself has lost much of what made her adorable. And while she may go on with the closed heart and become a saint, even saintship is hardly sufficient to compensate any man or woman for a half-lived life. The only thing worth doing in this world is to live life according to one's convictions—and one's heart. He or she who sells that fine independence for a mess of pottage, no matter if the mess be spiced, sells, as the Master said, the immortal part of him.

And so Lali, just here on the edge of Marion's future, looking into that mirror, was catching the reflection of her own life. When two women come so near that, like the lovers in the *Tempest*, they have changed eyes, in so far as to read each other's hearts,—even indifferently, which is much where two women are concerned, —there is only one resource, and that is to fall into each other's arms, and to weep if it be convenient, or to hold their tears for a more fitting occasion; and most people will admit that tears need not add to a bride's beauty. Marion might, therefore, be pardoned if she had her tears in her throat and not in her eyes, and Lali, if they arose for a moment no higher than her heart. But they did fall into each other's arms despite veils and orange blossoms, and somehow Marion had the feeling for Lali that she had on that first day at Greyhope, four years ago, when, standing on the bridge, the girl looked down into the water, tears dropping on her hands, and Marion said to her, " Poor girl ! poor girl ! " The situations were the same, because Lali had come to a new phase of her life, and what that phase would be who could tell—happiness or despair ?

The usual person might think that Lali was placing herself and her wifely affection at a rather high price, but then it is about the only thing that a woman can place high, even though she be one-third a white woman and two-thirds an Indian. Here was a beautiful woman, who had run the gamut of a London season, who had played a pretty social part, admirably trained therefor by one of the best and most cultured families of England. Besides, why should any woman sell her affections even to her husband, bargain away her love, the one thing that sanctifies "what God hath joined let no man put asunder"? Lali was primitive, she was unlike so many in a trivial world, but she was right. She might suffer, she might die, but, after all, there are many things worse than that. Man is born in a day, and he dies in a day, and the thing is easily over; but to have a sick heart for three-fourths of one's lifetime is simply to have death renewed every morning, and life at that price is not worth living. In this sensitive age we are desperately anxious to save life, as if it was the really great thing in the world ; but in the good, strong times of the earth—and in these times, indeed, when necessity knows its hour—men held their lives as lightly as a bird upon the housetop which any chance stone might drop.

It is possible that at this moment the two women understood each other better than they had ever done, and respected each other more. Lali, recovering herself, spoke a few soft words of congratulation, and then appeared to busy herself in putting little touches to Marion's dress, that soft persuasion of fingers which does so much to coax mere cloth into a sort of living harmony with the body.

They had no more words of confidence, but in the porch of the church, Marion, as she passed Lali, caught the slender fingers in her own and pressed them tenderly. Marion was giving comfort, and yet if she had been asked why she could not have told. She did not try to define it further than to say to herself that she herself was having almost too much happiness. The village was *en fête*, and peasants lined the street leading to the church, ready with their hearty God-bless-you's. Lali sat between her husband and Mrs. Armour, apparently impassive until there came the question, " *Who giveth this woman to be married to this man ?* " and General Armour's voice came clear and strong, "I do." Then a soft little cry broke from her, and she shivered slightly. Mrs. Armour did not notice, but Frank and Mrs. Lambert heard and saw, and both were afterwards watchful and solicitous. Frank caught Mrs. Lambert's eye, and it said, to a little motion of the head, "Do not appear to notice."

Lali was as if in a dream. She never took her eyes from the group at the altar until the end, and the two, now man and wife, turned to go into the vestry. Then she appeared to sink away into herself for a moment, before she fell into conversation with the others, as they moved towards the vestry.

"It was beautiful, wasn't it?" ventured Edward Lambert.

"The most beautiful wedding I ever saw," she answered, with a little shadow of meaning ; and Lambert guessed that it was the only one she had seen since she came to England.

"How well Vidall looked," said Frank, "and as proud as a sultan. Did you hear what he said, as Marion came up the aisle?"

"No," responded Lambert.

"He said, 'By Jove, isn't she fine!' He didn't seem conscious that other people were present."

"Well, if a man hasn't some inspirations on his wedding-day when *is* he to have them?" said Mrs. Lambert. "For my part, I think that the woman always does that sort of thing better than a man. It is her really great occasion, and she masters it—the comedy is all hers."

They were just then entering the vestry.

"Or the tragedy, as the case may be," said Lali quietly, smiling at Marion. She had, as it were, recovered herself, and her words had come with that airy, impersonal tone which permits nothing of what is said in it to be taken seriously. Something said by the others had recalled her to herself, and she was now returned very suddenly to the old position of alertness and social *finesse*. Something icy seemed to pass over her, and she immediately lost all self-consciousness, and began to speak to her husband with less reserve than she had shown since he had come. But he was not deceived. He saw that at that very instant she was further away from him than she had ever been. He sighed, in spite of himself, as Lali, with well-turned words, said some loving greetings to Marion, and then talked a moment with Captain Vidall.

"Who can understand a woman?" said Lambert to his wife meaningly.

"Whoever will," she answered.

" How do you mean ? "

" Whoever will wait like the saint upon the pillar, will suffer like the traveller in the desert ; serve like a slave, and demand like a king ; have patience greater than Job ; love ceaseless as a fountain in the hills ; who sees in the darkness and is not afraid of light ; who distrusts not, neither believes, but stands ready to be taught ; who is prepared for a kiss this hour and a reproach the next ; who turneth neither to right nor left at her words, but hath an unswerving eye—these shall understand a woman."

" I never knew you so philosophical. Where did you get this deliverance on the subject ? "

" May not even a woman have a moment of inspiration ? "

" I should expect that of my wife."

" And I should expect *that* of my husband. It is trite to say that men are vain ; I shall remark that they sit so much in their own light that they are surprised if another being crosses their disc."

" You always were clever, my dear, and you always were twice too good for me."

" Well, every woman—worth the knowing—is a missionary."

". Where does Lali come in ? "

" Can you ask ? To justify the claims of womanhood in spite of race—and all."

" To bring one man to a sense of the duty of sex to sex, eh ? "

" Truly. And is she not doing it well ? See her now."

They were now just leaving the church, and Lali had taken General Armour's arm, while Richard led his mother to the carriage.

Lali was moving with a little touch of grandeur in her manner and a more than ordinary deliberation. She had had a moment of great weakness, and then there had come the reaction—carried almost too far by the force of the will. She was indeed straining herself too far. Four years of tension were culminating.

"See her now, Edward," repeated Mrs. Lambert.

"Yes, but if I'm not mistaken, my dear, she is doing so well that she's going to pieces. She's overstrung to-day. If it were you, you'd be in hysterics."

" I believe you are right," was the grave reply. " There will be an end to this comedy one way or another very soon."

A moment afterwards they were in a carriage rolling away to Greyhope.

# CHAPTER XV

## THE END OF THE TRAIL

WHEN Marion was about starting away with her husband for the railway station, she came to Lali, who was standing half hidden by the curtains of a window, looking out at little Richard, who was parading his pony up and down before the house. An unutterable sweetness looked out of Marion's eyes. She had found, as it seemed to her, and as so many have believed until their lives' end, the secret of life. Lali saw the glistening joy, and responded to it, just as it was in her being to respond to every change of nature—that sensitiveness was in her as deep as life itself.

"You are very happy, dear?" she said to Marion.

"You cannot think how happy, Lali. And I want to say that I know, I feel sure, that you will be as happy, even happier than I. Oh, it will come—it will come. And you have the boy now—so fine, so good."

P 225

Lali looked out to where little Richard disported himself; her eyes shone, and she turned with a responsive but still sad smile to Marion. "Marion dear," she said gently, "the *other* should have come before *he* came."

"Frank loves you, dear."

"Who knows? And then, oh, I cannot tell! How can one force one's heart? No, no! One has to wait, and wait, even if the heart grows harder, and one gets hopeless."

Marion kissed her on the cheek and smiled. "Some day soon the heart will open up, and then such a flood will pour out. See, dear. I am going now, and our lives won't run together so much again ever, perhaps. But I want to tell you how that your coming to us has done me a world of good—helped me to be a wiser girl, and I ought to be a better woman for it. Good-bye."

They were calling to her, and with a hurried embrace they parted, and in a few moments the bride and bridegroom were on their way to the new life. As the carriage disappeared in a turn of the limes, Lali vanished also to her room. She was not seen at dinner. Mackenzie came to say that she was not very well, and that she would keep to her room. Frank sent several times during the evening to inquire after her, and was told that she was resting comfortably. He did not try to see her, and in this was wise. He had now fallen into a habit of delicate consideration, which brought its own reward. He had given up hope of winning her heart or confidence by storm, and had followed his finer and better instincts—had come to the point where he made no claims, and even in his own mind stood upon no rights. His mother brought him word from Lali, before he retired, to say that she was sorry she could not see him, but giving him a message and a commission into town the following morning for their son. Her tact had grown as her strength had declined. There is something in failing health—ill-health without disease—which sharpens and refines the faculties, and makes the temper exquisitely sensitive—that is, with people of a certain good sort. The *aplomb* and spirited manner in which Lali had borne herself at the wedding, and after, was the last flicker of her old strength, and of the second phase in her married life. The end of the first phase came with the ride at the quick-set hedge, this with a less intent but as active a temper.

The next morning she did not appear at breakfast, but sent a message to Frank to say that she was better, and adding another commission for town. All day, save for an hour on the balcony, she kept to her room, and lay down for the greater part of the afternoon. In the

227

evening, when Frank returned, his mother sent
for him, and frankly told him that she thought
it would be better for him to go away for a few
weeks or so; that Lali was in a languid, nervous
state, and she thought that by the time he got
back—if he would go—she would be better, and
that better things would come for him.

Frank was no longer the vain, selfish man
who had married Lali—something of the best
in him was at work. He understood, and suggested a couple of weeks with Richard at their
little place in Scotland. Frank saw his wife for
a little while that evening. She had been lying
down, but she disposed herself in a deep chair
before he entered. He was a little shocked to
see, as it were all at once, how delicate she
looked. He came and sat down near her, and
after a few moments of friendly talk, in which
he spoke solicitously of her health, he told her
that he thought of going up to Scotland with
Richard for a few weeks, if she saw no objection.

She did not quite understand why he was
going. She thought that perhaps he felt the
strain of the situation, and that a little absence
would be good for both. This pleased her.
She did not shrink, as she had so often done
since his return, when he laid his hand on hers
for an instant, as he asked her if she were
willing that he should go. Sometimes in the

past few weeks she had almost hated him. Now she was a little sorry for him, but she said that of course he must go ; that no doubt it was good that he should go, and so on, in gentle, allusive phrases. The next evening she came down to dinner, and was more like herself as she was before Frank came back, but she ate little, and before the men came into the drawing-room she had excused herself, and retired ; at which Mrs. Lambert shook her head apprehensively at herself, and made up her mind to stay at Greyhope longer than she intended.

Which was good for all concerned ; for, two nights after Frank and Richard had gone, Mackenzie hurried down to the drawing-room with the news that Lali had been found in a faint on her chamber floor. That was the beginning of weeks of anxiety, in which Mrs. Lambert was to Mrs. Armour what Marion would have been, and more ; and both to Lali all that mother and sister could be.

Their patient was unlike any other that they had known. Feverish, she had no fever ; with a gentle, hacking cough, she had no lung trouble ; nervous, she still was oblivious to very much that went on around her; hungering often for her child, she would not let him remain long with her when he came. Her sleep was broken, and she sometimes talked to herself, whether

229

consciously or unconsciously they did not know. The doctor had no remedies but tonics—he did not understand the case ; but he gently ventured the opinion that it was mostly a matter of race, that she was pining because civilisation had been infused into her veins—the old insufficient theory.

" Stuff and nonsense ! " said General Armour, when his wife told him. " The girl bloomed till Frank came back. God bless my soul ! she's falling in love, and doesn't know what it is."

He was only partly right, perhaps, but he was nearer the truth than the dealer in quinine and a cheap philosophy of life. " She'll come around all right, you'll see. Decline ?—decline be hanged ! The girl shall live,—damn it ! she shall ! " he blurted out, as his wife's eyes filled with tears.

Mrs. Lambert was much of the same mind as the general, but went further. She said to Mrs. Armour that in all her life she had never seen so sweet a character, so sensitive a mind—a mind whose sorrow was imagination. And therein the little lady showed herself a person of wisdom. For none of them had yet reckoned with that one great element in Lali's character—that thing which is the birthright of all who own the North for a mother, the awe of imagination, the awe and the pain, which in its finest expression comes near, very near, to the supernatural. Lali's mind was all pictures ; she never thought of things in words, she saw them ; and everything in her life arrayed itself in a scene before her, made vivid by her sensitive soul, so much more sensitive now with health failing, the spirit wearing out the body. There was her malady — the sick heart and mind.

A new sickness wore upon her. It had not touched her from the day she left the North until she sang " The Chase of the Yellow Swan " that first evening after Frank's return. Ever since then her father was much in her mind—the memory of her childhood, and its sweet, inspiring friendship with Nature. All the roughness and coarseness of the life was refined in her memory by the exquisite atmosphere of the North, the good sweet earth, the strong bracing wind, the *camaraderie* of trees and streams and grass and animals. And in it all stood her father, whom she had left alone, in that interminable interval between the old life and the new. Had she done right? She had cut him off, as if he had never been—her people, her country also; and for what? For this—for this sinking sense, this failing body, this wear and tear of mind and heart, this constant study to

231

be possible where she had once been declared
by the world to be impossible.

One night she lay sleeping after a rather
feverish day, when it was thought best to keep
the child from her. Suddenly she waked,
and sat up. Looking straight before her,
she said—

"*I will arise, and will go to my Father, and
will say unto Him, Father, I have sinned against
heaven and before Thee, and am no more worthy
to be called Thy son.*"

She said nothing more than this, and presently
lay back, with eyes wide open, gazing before
her. Like this she lay all night long, a strange,
aching look in her face. There had come upon
her the sudden impulse to leave it all, and go
back to her father. But the child—that gave
her pause. Towards morning she fell asleep,
and slept far on into the day, a thing that had
not occurred for a long time.

At noon a letter arrived for her. It came
into General Armour's hands, and he, seeing
that it bore the stamp of the Hudson's Bay
Company, with the legend, *From Fort St.
Charles*, concluded that it was news of Lali's
father. Then came the question whether the
letter should be given to her. The general was
for doing so, and he prevailed. If it were bad
news, he said, it might raise her out of her

present apathy and by changing the play of
her emotions do her good in the end.

The letter was given to her in the afternoon.
She took it apathetically, but presently, seeing
where it was from, she opened it hurriedly with
a little cry which was very like a moan too.
There were two letters inside—one from the
factor at Fort Charles in English, and one from
her father in the Indian language. She read
her father's letter first, the other fluttered to her
feet from her lap. General Armour, looking
down, saw a sentence in it which, he felt,
warranted him in picking it up, reading it,
and retaining it, his face settling into painful
lines as he did so. Days afterwards, Lali read
her father's letter to Mrs. Armour. It ran :—

My daughter,

Lali, the sweet noise of the Spring :

Thy father speaks.

I have seen more than half a hundred moons
come like the sickle and go like the eye of a
running buck, swelling with fire, but I hear not
thy voice at my tent door since the first one
came and went.

*Thou art gone.*

Thy face was like the sun on running water ;
thy hand hung on thy wrists like the ear of a

young deer; thy foot was as soft on the grass
as the rain on a child's cheek; thy words were
like snow in summer, which melts in richness
on the hot earth. Thy bow and arrow hang
lonely upon the wall, and thy empty cup is
beside the pot.

*Thou art gone.*

Thou hast become great with a great race,
and that is well. Our race is not great, and
shall not be, until the hour when the Mighty
Men of the Kimash Hills arise from their sleep
and possess the land again.

*Thou art gone.*

But thou hast seen many worlds, and thou
hast learned great things, and thou and I shall
meet no more; for how shall the wise kneel at
the feet of the foolish, as thou didst kneel once
at thy father's feet?

*Thou art gone.*

High on the Clip Claw Hills the trees are
green, in the Plain of the Rolling Stars the
wings of the wild fowl are many, and fine is the
mist upon Goldfly Lake; and the heart of Eye-
of-the Moon is strong.

*Thou art here.*

The trail is open to the White Valley, and
the Scarlet Hunter hath saved me, when my
feet strayed in the plains and my eyes were
blinded.

*Thou art here.*

I have friends on the Far Off River who show me the yards where the musk-ox gather; I have found the gardens of the young sable, and my tents are full of all manner of store.

*Thou art here.*

In the morning my spirit is light, and I have harvest where I would gather, and the stubble is for my foes. In the evening my limbs are heavy, and I am at rest in my blanket. The hunt is mine and sleep is mine, and my soul is cheerful when I remember thee.

*Thou art here.*

I have built for thee a place where thy spirit comes. I hear thee when thou callest to me, and I go and kneel outside the door, for thou art wise, and thou speakest to me; but thee as thou art in a far land I shall see no more. This is my word to thee, that thou mayst know that I am not alone. Thou shalt not come again, as thou once went; it is not meet. But by these other ways I will speak to thee.

*Thou art here.*

Farewell. I have spoken.

Lali finished reading, and then slowly folded up the letter. The writing was that of the wife of the factor at Fort Charles — she knew it. She sat for a minute looking straight before

her. She read her father's allegory. Barbarian
in so much as her father was, he had beaten this
thing out with the hammer of wisdom. He
missed her, but she must not come back; she
had outgrown the old life—he knew it  and she
was with him in spirit, in his memory; she
understood his picturesque phrases, borrow'd
from the large, affluent world about him. Something of the righteousness and magnanimity of
this letter passed into her, giving her for an
instant a sort of peace. She had needed it—
needed it to justify herself, and she had been
justified. To return was impossible—she had
known that all along, though she had not
admitted it; the struggle had been but a kind
of remorse, after all. That her father should
come to her was also impossible—it was neither
for her happiness nor his. She had been two
different persons in her life, and the first was
only a memory to the second. The father had
solved the problem for her. He too was now a
memory that she could think on with pleasure, as
associated with the girl she once was. He had
been well provided for by her husband, and——

General Armour put his hand on hers gently
and said—

"Lali, without your permission I have read
this other letter."

She did not appear curious. She was thinking still of her father's letter to her. She nodded abstractedly.

"Lali," he continued, "this says that your father wished that letter to be written to you just as he spoke it at the Fort on the day of the Feast of the Yellow Swan. He stood up—the factor writes so here—and said that he had been thinking much for years, and that the time had come when he must speak to his daughter over the seas"—

General Armour paused. Lali inclined her head, smiled wistfully, and held up the letter for him to see. The general continued—

"So he spoke as has been written to you, and then they had the Feast of the Yellow Swan, and that night"— He paused again, but presently, his voice a little husky, he went on: "That night he set out on a long journey,"— he lifted the letter and looked at it, then met the serious eyes of his daughter-in-law,—"on a long journey to the Hills of the Mighty Men; and, my dear, he never came back; for, as he said, there was peace in the White Valley, and he would rest till the world should come to its Spring again, and the noise of its coming should be in his ears. Those, Lali, are his very words."

His hand closed on hers, he reached out and took the other hand, from which the paper

237

fluttered, and clasped both tight in his own firm grasp.

"My daughter," he said, "you have another father."

With a low cry, like that of a fawn struck in the throat, she slid forward on her knees beside him, and buried her face on his arm. She understood. Her father was dead. Mrs. Armour came forward, and, kneeling also, drew the dark head to her bosom. Then that flood came which sweeps away the rust that gathers in the eyes and breaks through the closed dikes of the heart.

Hours after, when she had fallen into a deep sleep, General Armour and his wife met outside her bedroom door.

"I shall not leave her," Mrs. Armour said. "Send for Frank. His time has almost come."

But it would not have come so soon had not something else occurred. The day that he came back from Scotland he entered his wife's room, prepared for a change in her, yet he did not find so much to make him happy as he had hoped. She received him with a gentleness which touched him, she let her hand rest in his, she seemed glad to have him with her. All bars had been cast down between them, but he knew that she had not given him all, and she knew it

238

also. But she hoped he did not know, and she dreaded the hour when he would speak out of his now full heart. He did not yet urge his affection on her, he was simply devoted, and watchful, and tender, and delightedly hopeful.

But one night she came tapping at his door. When he opened it, she said, "Oh come, come! Our Richard is ill! I have sent for the doctor."

Henceforth she was her old self again, with a transformed spirit, her motherhood spending itself in a thousand ways. She who was weak bodily became now much stronger; the light of new vigour came to her eyes; she and her husband, in the common peril, worked together, thinking little of themselves, and all of the child. The last stage of the journey to happiness was being passed, and if it was not obvious to themselves, the others, Marion and Captain Vidall included, saw it.

One anxious day, after the family doctor had left the sick child's room, Marion, turning to the father and mother, said, "Greyhope will be itself again. I will go and tell Richard that the danger is over."

As she turned to do so, Richard entered the room. " I have seen the doctor," he began, "and the little chap is going to pull along like a house afire."

Tapping Frank affectionately on the arm, he

was about to continue, but he saw what stopped him. He saw the last move in Frank Armour's tragic-comedy. He and Marion left the room as quickly as was possible to him, for, as he said himself, he was "slow at a quick march"; and a moment afterwards the wife heard without demur her husband's tale of love for her.

Yet, as if to remind him of the wrong he had done, Heaven never granted Frank Armour another child.

**THE END.**